Somebody Else's Summer

Also by Jean Little

Somebody Else's Summer

JEAN LITTLE

VIKING
CANADA

VIKING CANADA

Published by the Penguin Group

Penguin Group (Canada), 90 Eglinton Avenue East, Suite 700, Toronto, Ontario,
Canada M4P 2Y3 (a division of Pearson Penguin Canada Inc.)

Penguin Group (USA) Inc., 375 Hudson Street, New York, New York 10014, U.S.A.
Penguin Books Ltd, 80 Strand, London WC2R 0RL, England
Penguin Ireland, 25 St Stephen's Green, Dublin 2, Ireland (a division of Penguin Books Ltd)
Penguin Group (Australia), 250 Camberwell Road, Camberwell, Victoria 3124, Australia
(a division of Pearson Australia Group Pty Ltd)
Penguin Books India Pvt Ltd, 11 Community Centre, Panchsheel Park,
New Delhi – 110 017, India
Penguin Group (NZ), cnr Airborne and Rosedale Roads, Albany, Auckland 1310,
New Zealand (a division of Pearson New Zealand Ltd)
Penguin Books (South Africa) (Pty) Ltd, 24 Sturdee Avenue, Rosebank, Johannesburg 2196,
South Africa

Penguin Books Ltd, Registered Offices: 80 Strand, London WC2R 0RL, England

First published 2005

1 2 3 4 5 6 7 8 9 10 (RRD)

LIBRARY AND ARCHIVES CANADA CATALOGUING IN PUBLICATION

Little, Jean, 1932–
Somebody else's summer / Jean Little.

ISBN 0-670-04466-0

I. Title.

PS8523.I77S62   2005   jC813'.54   C2005-900215-8

Visit the Penguin Group (Canada) website at **www.penguin.ca**

This story is for Sara Smith, with my love

Somebody Else's Summer

1

The two girls caught sight of each other at exactly the same moment. They were both lined up at the Air Canada counter but, until Alex's mother moved forward, Alex had been hidden behind her. Sam was taller than her tiny grandmother so she could see over her head with no problem. For a split second, the girls stared at each other. Then they both looked away fast.

"I hope that wimpy little kid isn't on my flight," Sam muttered in her grandmother's ear. "She looks as though she'll cry all the way."

Grandma's eyes followed Sam's. Then she frowned at her granddaughter.

"Samantha Cecily Scott, have a heart," she said. "I do see what you mean but appearances can be misleading. Look at the two of us!"

Sam grinned. Heaven knew what the other kid would think looking at them. Grandma was all dressed up to go into hospital. She was to have her hip surgery the day after tomorrow. Sam, on the other hand, was in her oldest jeans and a T-shirt covered with giant sunflowers. Her feet were shoved into battered sandals and her unruly black curls were cut short for the summer. Even if she was going to be stuck hanging around a bookstore, she wanted to feel free. When her hair grew long, it was a great nuisance. People were forever after her to do something to tame it.

The other girl was wearing all the most expensive kid things. Brand new, too. Sam could actually see the price tag on her pants. Her shoes were so clean they could not have been worn more than once or twice. She wore a vest that matched her pants and a greenish brown turtleneck which, Sam bet, matched her eyes. Her mother, if that was her mother, was also so fashionable she made Sam blink. Even the father was as neat as a new pin.

"Would you call him a dandy?" she muttered at Grandma.

"Trying hard anyway," Grandma agreed. "The girl looks wretched, though, Sam. If you get a chance, don't play tough guy; be kind."

"Have mercy, Grandma," Sam said. "I'm not a babysitter. She looks like a seven-year-old."

"And you look like a teenager—but you aren't. Give her a chance. I'll bet she's at least nine."

Sam rolled her eyes in mock horror.

"Maybe I won't even meet her," she said hopefully. "I don't want to listen to her whine."

"Sam, stop showing your mean streak," Grandma said.

Then the line moved forward and she forgot the little misery.

"Is she travelling unaccompanied?" the woman behind the counter asked Grandma.

"If you mean me," Sam muttered, "I am."

She hated being talked about as if she were not only deaf but invisible. Under the counter, Grandma gave Sam a poke.

"Yes, she is," Grandma told the woman in a worried voice. "Someone will be meeting her in Toronto, though."

They gave Grandma a sign to hang around Sam's neck announcing to the world that she was an unaccompanied minor. Sam was mortified. She pretended it was not dangling there, singling her out. The other girl had one hung on her front too.

"If you'll just be seated on the bench there, an agent will come to escort you onto the aircraft," the lady said, looking to see who was next in line.

Sam and Grandma sat.

"If only I could have reached your father," Grandma said.

"Stop it," Sam told her. "It'll be fine. You said so yourself. A real adventure, you said. And you'd spoil Dad's fun for nothing."

She smiled as she spoke but inside she was not feeling one bit adventuresome. If only her father had not chosen this summer to join a dig in the wilds of South America. He was supposed to be researching his next book there but Sam knew he'd also gone along purely for the fun of it.

"I'll stay with one of your friends until you're well again," Sam had offered, when Grandma got an unexpected chance to have her surgery. How was Sam to guess that the friend her grandmother would choose would live not in Nanaimo but in Ontario?

"You'll love Margaret Trueblood. I wish I could go too. I'd love to see her again," Grandma kept saying. "It's been years."

Ha!

"I'm sorry but I don't think I'll be up to letter-writing, sweetheart. Once I'm out of hospital, I'm going to be staying with Gladys while I have therapy. I'll write when I can but don't worry if you don't hear for a month or so."

"I won't," Sam said, only half-listening. Her father had told her he couldn't write to her either. He didn't even have a mailing address. Sam was not accustomed to getting letters from either of them so could not imagine getting into a state over not getting mail.

"If something goes wrong," she said suddenly, "will Aunt Gladys tell me?"

Her grandmother laughed and patted her hand.

"If you don't hear, I'm fine," she said. "But someone will let Margaret Trueblood know if there is any kind of emergency."

Reassured, Sam sat back and looked sideways at the other girl.

She was now perched at the far end of the bench. Her mother and father had not stayed with her, which surprised Sam. Had they been in such a hurry they couldn't even wait to say goodbye? It looked like they'd just dumped her and taken off. Sam felt a small twinge of pity despite herself.

She could not know that Alex had been glad when Perry had refused to wait.

"Alexis will be fine now and we have a lot to do, remember, Zelda," he had said, patting his stepdaughter's shoulder with a beefy hand, and then reaching to draw his wife away.

"But Perry," the woman had objected feebly.

Just then, the Air Canada agent had approached them.

"Don't worry, sir. We'll take good care of your little girl," the agent had said.

Alex had opened her mouth to say she was not Perry's little girl but let it go. She'd been afraid she might burst into tears. She had raised her face for her mother's hasty kiss and turned away. Now she sat where she'd been put and studied the girl in the sunflower shirt. That must be her grandmother with her. You could tell they loved each other. Alex swallowed.

Then another agent arrived. "Come with me," the agent said. "It's time to go through Security."

He seated them in the departure lounge and they ignored each other. Time ticked by. Both girls struggled to look relaxed, as if they flew on a daily basis. Neither quite pulled it off.

"Will anyone needing to be pre-boarded please make yourself known to the agent at this time," a disembodied voice said, naming their flight number.

Sam and Alex both got to their feet. A mother with a baby and a man with a Seeing Eye dog also rose but no other children joined them. Sam's heart sank.

Help! I'm going to have to sit with her, she moaned inwardly. She was absolutely right.

2

When the flight attendant seated Sam and Alex side by side, they were still careful to avoid looking at each other. They were sure they had nothing in common, and neither was in the mood to talk. Both were anxious, and both were determined not to let it show.

Alex was small for ten. She had brown hair and grey-green eyes hidden behind large glasses. She stared out the window at the wing and struggled not to think of her cat, Mercury. It was crazy. Merc had been put to sleep over two months ago. Her mother had taken him to the vet with Alex the morning after her stepfather, Perry, came home to announce that he had agreed to make a speech at a conference in Australia in July and he had ordered the tickets already.

"We can bring wives but not children," he had said firmly, not looking at Alex. "But I'm sure we can find someplace for Allie to stay while we're away."

"What about Merc?" she had cried, knowing as she did what the answer would be.

"It's high time that animal went to Kitty Heaven," Perry had muttered. "He's positively disgusting."

Alex had opened her mouth to scream at him but ran away to her bedroom instead. Protesting would have done no good. Her mother had wanted to get rid of the old cat from the moment they had moved to the townhouse, where everything was glossy and smooth and decorated in beige. Merc had had scant energy for scratching fabrics into shreds by then but he still shed gobs of hair and, when Alex lifted him onto a couch or bed and he napped there, he occasionally dribbled a bit when he first stood up again. He had had bad breath, too, and he had been practically blind.

"You don't want him to suffer," Mum had said. "Alex, he must be almost twenty years old."

She did not really know Merc's age. He had already been an adult cat when he had appeared on Dad's doorstep before Alex's parents were married. She could not remember life without him. Dad had insisted on adopting him. Alex herself, in her secret heart, admitted that the cat had grown less and less appealing in the last year or so. But he still recognized her, purring wheezily whenever she stroked him and lifting his big head every time she called him by name.

"Alex is your baby," Dad had told Mum, "and Mercury is mine."

But Merc had followed Alex around and allowed himself to be played with as though he were a stuffed toy. And, when Mum and Dad had split up three years ago, Dad had given his cat to his daughter as a farewell present. Mum had been angry but she had not been hard-hearted enough to have her child's cat put to sleep immediately after she had lost her beloved father. Mercury had been elderly even then but not ill. He was clearly ill now.

Alex had stayed with him when he was given the lethal injection. He had protested at the needle prick but the doctor had been deft and it was over in a few seconds. Turning to go, she had blinked away the tears that blurred her last sight of him. If it had not been for Perry's moving in with them, she could have accepted Merc's death, knowing he was ready to go. But as it was, it gave her one more outrage to lay at Perry's door.

Alex was surprised and puzzled even yet by the speed with which her mother and Perry had thrown themselves into planning this trip. The wedding had been in March. The three of them had lived together in Mum's apartment at first. Then Perry had found a condominium that was "made for us."

Since then, Mum and Perry had said things to each other about Sydney and Brisbane but Alex had not paid much attention until the day Mum had said she'd better get some new clothes for the trip.

"What trip?" Alex had asked. She knew, really, but she had pushed it to the very back of her mind and almost erased it from her memory.

"Perry told you. He and I are going to Australia for July and August," her mother had said, looking away. "He has a conference to go to, remember? Wives are invited, but not children."

"Australia!" Alex had echoed, feeling hollow.

"Don't play games, miss. You know all about it," Mum had said too loudly. "It's the chance of a lifetime. We've made no secret of it."

"Where will I be?" Alex had asked.

"Wilderness camp," her mother had said, not looking at her. "You'll love it. They go canoeing and camp out under the stars."

Alex had no wish to canoe or sleep under the stars, but it turned out that the camp was cancelled at the last moment because not enough campers had signed up.

Then, out of the blue, her mother had got a flyer in the mail advertising Heron Hill Horse Farm. It had come from an old school friend of Mum's, someone Alex had never met, someone she had never even heard of before.

"She must have mailed them out to everyone on her Christmas card list," Mum had said. "Hallelujah! I would never have thought of her but it sounds absolutely perfect."

She had called Guelph that very evening and Mary Grantham, the lady who had sent the flyer, had agreed to take Alex in.

"She'll have to share a room with Bethany," she had said, "but if you'll pay her board ... We certainly could do with a paying guest."

Alex had been eavesdropping on the upstairs phone. At the thought of the unknown roommate, her heart plummeted. Then she heard her mother gush, "Oh, Alex will be so thrilled. She's mad about horses, you know!"

At this out-and-out lie, Alex had hung up, not caring if the other woman heard. Did Mum really believe she was mad about horses? She couldn't. Alex was terrified of the great clopping things with their alarming speed and towering height. She had never ridden one, never wanted to.

She tried to talk to her mother but it did no good. Zelda had arranged everything and was pleased as punch about it.

"You'll feel differently when you've learned to ride" was all she would say.

"Dad wouldn't make me go." Alex tried one last desperate attempt to rescue herself from a nightmare summer.

"Your father is not here, in case you haven't noticed," her mother had snapped, and then she walked away from the discussion.

When Zelda had married Jon Kennedy, she had thought it was romantic to be married to an artist who was trying to make a living as a painter. But once Alex was born, there never seemed to be enough money.

"No pension plan," Zelda had stormed at Jon. "No dental plan. No security."

Finally she had put Alex in daycare and started taking courses in money management. When her career was growing by leaps and bounds and Jon was still struggling, she had laid down her ultimatum.

"Give up working as an artist for peanuts and get a real job or leave," she had told him.

Seven-year-old Alex had lain curled up on her bed listening and praying that he would not go, but he finally did.

And now he had left British Columbia and was working part time as an art teacher in Toronto. He had written to her faithfully until Zelda married Perry. Then, all at once, the letters had stopped. Alex did not even know exactly where he lived now. She had written to tell him of Merc's death and Zelda had taken the letter to mail but he had not written back. It was not like him but she had not brought it up. Zelda would have started saying abusive things about him, and his daughter, who loved him more than anyone, could not bear it.

As she sat remembering all this, the plane took off in a great rush of sound and Vancouver was left behind.

"Would you like something to drink, dear?" the flight attendant asked Sam.

"Um … orange juice, please," Sam muttered.

Alex turned, knowing she would be next.

"Nothing," she said without waiting to be asked.

Sam glanced at her, taking in the straight brown hair and bangs, the large glasses, and the drooping mouth. Then the girl lifted her chin and Sam saw the wide grey-green eyes that the spectacles had hidden. The eyes were unexpectedly lovely but they had been crying. Well, maybe not crying but on the verge. Her eyelids were suspiciously pink.

"Did anyone introduce you two? Sam Scott and … Alex Kennedy, is it?"

They nodded, not meeting each other's eyes.

"Are you both going to Ontario for a visit?" the woman asked.

When Alex remained stubbornly silent, Sam said, "Sort of. My dad's away for the summer and I'm being sent to stay with a friend of my grandmother's in a place called Guelph. I've never met her even though she was my mum's godmother and she doesn't know me, but I'm not what she's expecting."

She didn't know why she added that. Next to her, the crybaby stiffened with a jerk and shot her a surprised glance.

"How about you?" the nosy woman asked.

Alex hesitated. Then she blurted out, "I'm going to Guelph too, and the people I'm going to stay with don't know me either. They have a bunch of kids and a stable." Then, like Sam, she added the part that disturbed her most. "That lady is in for a shock too. She thinks I'm crazy about horses. She couldn't be more wrong."

The flight attendant seemed to think this incredibly funny. She threw back her head and laughed, but before she could pump Alex for more information somebody pressed a call button and she moved up the aisle.

Alex slumped back in her seat and shut her eyes. She was not in the mood to stare at clouds. Just the thought of meeting the total strangers who were going to take her in for the summer made her stomach squirm.

"That is so weird," the girl beside her said. "That's incredible. I can't believe it."

Alex was annoyed. She was not a talkative girl and she was not in the mood to chat. She kept her eyes shut but she could tell the other girl was still staring right into her face. Finally, she opened her eyes wide and glared back.

"I don't see what's so incredible," she snapped. "We're both going to a place called Guelph. So what? It's a coincidence, that's all."

The other girl wore no glasses and her eyes were as blue as the sky on a crisp October day. Her short, curly black hair stood on end as though she had been running her hands through it.

"Coincidence maybe," Sam said. "But also amazing. Listen and I'll tell you. I'm being sent to a college friend of my grandma's. She and her husband run a second-hand bookshop. They all think I love reading because my father pushes books at me morning, noon, and night. I pretend I like them but I really like playing sports better. I would love to go where I could ride horses. I've always wanted lessons but we can't afford them. What's more, I've never met my people either. So we're in the same boat. That's what's incredible."

*A*lex twisted until she was facing Sam. She no
longer looked small and wretched. She no longer
looked bored and snooty either. Behind her
glasses, her eyes were ablaze with fellow feeling.

"I'm supposed to call mine 'aunt' even though I've never
met her. I'll have to share Bethany's bedroom. What do you
bet she's only seven or eight!"

Sam blinked.

"How old are you?" she asked, not looking Alex straight
in the eye.

Alex read her thoughts and glared again.

"I'll be eleven on Halloween," she said. "I suppose that
seems young to you but ..."

Sam laughed aloud.

"I'll be eleven on Guy Fawkes Day, November 5," she said. "Is this amazing or isn't it? We're practically twins."

"I thought you were at least thirteen," Alex said.

Sam did not say how old she had guessed Alex was. Neither of them knew what to say for the next few seconds. They sat, trying to take in what each other had spilled out and make sense of it. Then Sam spoke in hushed tones.

"Horses," she breathed. "You're going to a place with horses? Are you ever lucky!"

Alex's face went as blank as a hard-boiled egg.

"I hate horses," she said, half under her breath. "They're five miles tall and they have teeth like tombstones. And these people are going to want me to ride. They said I'd adore it."

"You're out of your mind," Sam told her. "It sounds like a dream come true to me! My dad couldn't afford riding lessons for me. He is a freelance writer. He's not famous or anything. He writes travel articles and he's just had his first murder mystery published. It's a computer mystery and it's called *Fatal Error*."

Alex thought of telling the girl about her father but she thought better of it. None of his work had been a big success. She grinned, pushing her glasses up on her nose and smiling through them. "Cool title," she said.

Sam studied her. Should she tell about the character called Sam in her father's book? No. Not yet.

"Yeah," she agreed. "He's working on another one. The first one is dedicated to me. It says, 'For Sam, who done it.' Don't ask me what it means. He just laughed when I asked."

"Hey, that's neat," Alex said, impressed.

"It sounds good but we never, never have enough money for stuff like riding lessons. Grandma's frequent flyer points paid for my plane ticket."

Alex looked out the window. Perry was a dental surgeon and her mother was a financial advisor. Not only could she have riding lessons if she wanted them, but she could probably have her very own horse someday. As a matter of fact, they would be happy as skylarks if she'd suggested such a thing. They wanted her to stop being a bookworm and work on something that would make her bring home an Olympic gold. Her mother was sports crazy. She sat glued to the TV, watching the figure skaters, the skiers, the curlers. She had had Alex learn to figure-skate at four but Alex had kept sprawling on the ice. Alex had gone on to be a flop at every sport her mother could come up with—ballet, gymnastics, judo, skiing, soccer. Dad had told Mum to give up but no way. Alex had been taking golfing lessons when Perry came along and distracted her mother for a while.

Then Perry had taken up the challenge, only his thing was technology. Alex should get into surfing the World Wide Web like other techno wizards. Seeing her reading *Harry*

Potter and the Prisoner of Azkaban for the third time had made her stepfather throw up his hands and cry, "Why on earth are you wasting your time reading some silly story you already know by heart?"

Alex had wanted to say Harry Potter was her friend, which was the truth. Instead she said coolly, "I'm studying the writer's technique. After all, she's making millions writing these 'silly' stories."

A small satisfied smile flickered across her mouth as she remembered Perry's confusion. He never read fiction but he had tremendous respect for money.

"I'll bet this stable is too far from the public library for me to walk there," she said glumly.

Sam laughed.

"Listen to this. My lady and her husband actually own a bookstore," she said. "I've never met her but that's what my grandmother said. I'd like to get away from reading for a bit but fat chance. My father is, of course, mad about books. I'm a big disappointment to him. Well, maybe not. But I would be if he guessed how tired I get of reading about ancient ruins and olden-day kings and stuff. I have to pretend."

"How about your mother?" Alex asked, fascinated.

"She's dead," Sam said cheerfully.

Alex's eyes widened even more and she flushed with embarrassment.

Sam laughed.

"Don't worry. I don't remember her. We were in a car crash when I was one. She got killed but I was protected by my car seat and came out without a scratch. I don't remember her at all."

"What happened to you afterwards?" Alex asked.

"My grandma came to live with us for a while but, when I was old enough to go to daycare, she went back to running her bed and breakfast in Nanaimo. This old friend of hers wrote to her just when she was needing someone to look after me while she had her hip replaced. 'I could stay with one of your friends,' I told her. Next thing I knew, the two of them had it all arranged. We lived so far away that I think this Margaret Trueblood had forgotten I existed. She was my mother's godmother, though, so she felt a bit responsible."

Alex thought briefly of her own mother, who only read money magazines and cookbooks. But she jerked her thoughts away from mothers as she realized something astonishing. She hesitated for one moment longer. Then she spoke the startling idea aloud.

"You know what? If we switched, they'd never notice. Then you could ride the horses and I could read the books."

Sam was struck dumb for a full twenty seconds. Then she said, "What?"

Alex repeated herself. Sam could not believe her ears but she said, "You're crazy but … maybe you're right! They would have no way of knowing. Wow!"

4

They sat in total silence for a full minute, thinking.

"It would be fun to try," Alex said in a whisper.

"Yeah," Sam said, lowering her voice. "But I don't have that much nerve. We'd never be able to pull it off."

"Well, I think we might," Alex said slowly. "Not for long, maybe. But it would be neat if we could do it. Even for a week or two. It would be worth it. What could they do to us?"

"Charge us with fraud," Sam shot back, but she was smiling.

They sat in thoughtful silence until breakfast was brought to them. After that, there was a movie.

Then Sam burst out, "Let's pretend we're going to try it and plan how we'd manage. First of all, let's give each other addresses and phone numbers and any information we have. Then, if we get mail for each other, we can forward it. We can plan out lots of stuff like that."

She dug out a small notepad her grandmother had given her and copied the Truebloods' address. Alex watched with interest and then followed suit.

"Now," said Alex, "here's mine."

"Hey, look," Sam said, holding out the two sheets of paper side by side, "our handwriting is so alike you couldn't tell which was which."

"Both messy," said Alex, grinning. But Sam was right. Their writing was nearly identical.

Alex began to plan again.

"I'll call you Alex for the rest of the trip and you can call me Sam."

The flight attendant, who had left them looking glummer than glum, was pleased to see the pair of them giggling over something. She smiled to herself and nodded her head. She had known all along that children made friends easily. She would never have believed what they were really up to.

It was just a game, of course, invented to pass the time, and yet underneath their laughter there was an intense longing. By the time they had flown from Manitoba into Ontario, they were feeling comfortable with their new names and hardly ever slipping up.

When the plane landed in Toronto and they followed the agent to where they were to meet their hosts, each of them had the other's address and phone number as well as her own. They had described their luggage. Then, remembering how different they looked, they agreed they would need to get their own suitcases despite the giveaway labels.

"It shouldn't be all that hard to do. We can distract them somehow," Sam said. But she had a cold, sickish feeling in the pit of her stomach and she was sure, if anyone was checking, that her hands would shake like a dog in a thunderstorm.

When the moment actually arrived, however, they did not have to do anything too tricky. After all, they were the only children travelling independently. The people had a fifty-percent chance of guessing right.

"Are you Sam?" a very tall old woman called, hurrying up to Alex. "I knew it. You get your bag and I'll find a cart. The car is waiting. I'm in a bit of a rush."

"Hello, Alex darling," called a much shorter, younger woman with a weather-beaten face and very blond hair cut short. She had kids of assorted sizes grouped around her, all of whom were staring at Sam with wide brown eyes. Sam was fascinated to see that no two were the same shade. The boy's were like a peeled chestnut, the little girl's like chocolate, and the tall girl's much lighter, like weak tea maybe, and their mother's were the colour of the sherry Dad kept to give Grandma when she came to visit.

"Welcome to Ontario." The woman's overly hearty voice broke in on Sam's thoughts. "Can we help you with your luggage?"

"I'll help her," shrieked the small girl. "Let me. *Pul-leaze!* I never get to do anything."

"You can't read well enough, Josie," the older girl, who was probably Bethany, said crushingly, tossing her ponytail. "What help could you possibly be? Get a grip."

Sam saw Alex, at the baggage carousel, grab both their bags. She must be ripping the labels off, just as they had said they would.

"Josie can help," she said loudly. "Come on, Josie. You're all the help I need."

Josie's face lit up like a jack-o'-lantern and she trotted after Sam. By the time the two of them had reached Alex's side, she had seen to it that no name tags identified their bags.

"Last chance to back out," she murmured as her eyes met Sam's. She, too, was trembling.

"Not me," Sam said, doing her best to sound cool and collected. "Here you go, Josie."

Josie, clutching Sam's tote bag, trundled off toward her mother while the two older girls kept murmuring. Josie was so proud of helping the visitor she did not really notice Alex.

"Remember those horses. Write to me, though. We can call each other once we know it's safe. If it isn't long distance."

Alex glanced over at the old woman, skinny as a string bean and tall as a tree, who had called her Sam. She had stopped to speak to the Grantham family! They must know each other. Help! What were they saying? No, it was fine. Mrs. Trueblood was turning away and looking for Alex again.

"Let's go, Sam," she called. "We've got an hour's drive ahead of us and I have to get home."

She strode away, not even checking to make sure her guest was following. Alex gulped and then smiled shakily at Samantha.

"Good luck, Alex Kennedy," she said with a catch in her throat.

She waited to see the shock register on Sam's face and to hear her gasp. She was not disappointed. Sam stood stock-still, gazing goggle-eyed at her. Mrs. Trueblood would be out of sight in a minute. Snatching up the strap that pulled her suitcase, Alex dashed after the total stranger with whom she was supposed to spend the rest of the summer.

"Good luck yourself, Sam Scott," she heard Sam call.

For a split second, Alex longed to race up to one of the women and confess. The thought of keeping up such a complicated deception scared her. If they backed out right now, everybody would take it as a practical joke and let it pass. They might be annoyed but they would not ship the two of them back to British Columbia. She felt like someone setting forth across a field sown with land mines. Any minute the whole thing was going to blow sky-high.

"Come on, Sam," Margaret Trueblood called back to her.

Alex closed her mouth and took her first step into the adventure.

*S*am found that the Grantham family had moved nearer while she and Alex were talking. They were not close enough to have overheard anything puzzling, though. Josie was too young to have made sense of Alex's guarded words. Everyone but Bethany was grinning at her, even Mrs. Grantham. Bethany looked as though she'd swallowed a sour pickle by mistake and it was stuck halfway down.

Sam felt panic tremble through her whole body. She had turned to jelly and she was shaking and she couldn't stop. Yet nobody appeared to notice. So she jammed her hands deep in her pockets and plastered a wide fake smile on her face and waited for someone else to make the first move.

"We didn't even introduce ourselves properly," the mother said. "I'm Mary, of course. You can call me Aunt Mary. That way, we'll feel related. This is Bethany, who's going to be your roommate while you're with us. The middle one is Kenneth. And Josie is the seven-year-old. We also have a baby at home. He's five and his name is Thomas. We left him at home so we would have enough room in the van for you and your luggage. Besides, he despises long car rides."

Sam knew, instantly, that baby Thomas was the apple of his mother's eye and she felt sorry for Josie, who was a gangly child, all elbows and big new teeth. Kenneth seemed fine. He grinned at her as though he meant it. Bethany still looked as though she'd like to erase Sam from the world.

"Hi," Sam said stiffly, letting her glance slide swiftly over all of them without stopping to look closely at any one.

"Do you have a brother, Alex?" Mary Grantham asked.

It took Sam a moment to realize that she was the person being addressed. Then she scrambled around in her mind trying to remember what Alex had said about her family. Only child. That was it. Just like her.

"Not one," she said. "There's just me, my mother, and my stepfather, Terry."

"Terry? I thought Zelda called him Perry," the woman said. "I always get names wrong."

"It's because you don't listen," Bethany said sharply. She sounded incredibly rude. Grandma would never have let Sam speak to her in such a sneering way. But then, she would not want to speak to Grandma like that. She loved her grandmother. Did Bethany hate her mother or was she being mean for some other reason? Sam stared at the older girl thoughtfully. Bethany flushed and glared at her mother. "Or maybe you're just going deaf," she added.

Mary Grantham glanced at her daughter. Sam saw hurt in her eyes. But the woman did her best to laugh it off.

"Could be," she said.

"His name *is* Perry," Sam said hurriedly. "It came out wrong, I guess."

They marched in a body to the parking lot and there wasn't a chance for any more awkward questions. Sam wanted to mop her brow but resisted.

The minute the van doors were unlocked, Bethany pushed past Sam to get into the front seat as if it were her rightful place.

"I was going to ask Alex if she'd like to ride up front," Mary Grantham said but, when Bethany ignored her, she shrugged and said, "Maybe you'd prefer to sit with the others, Alex."

"Sure would," Sam said in her sweetest voice.

Swiftly, she climbed into the middle seat next to Josie. Kenneth got into the seat behind and leaned forward to hiss in Sam's ear.

"Ignore her. She's being an obnoxious teenager and she wants us to notice."

Sam gave him a quick grin and pretended Bethany had fallen over a cliff.

Once the van door was hauled shut, she took her first deep breath since the plane had touched down.

As seat belts snapped into place, Kenneth spoke right out loud.

"Is your name short for Alexandra?" he asked.

"Alexis," Sam muttered, staring out the window and praying she had it right.

"How pretty," Aunt Mary said, turning the key in the ignition.

Sam, desperate to avoid any more dangerous subjects, asked a question of her own.

"How many horses do you have?"

Suddenly Bethany became a different girl.

"Fourteen," she said, twisting around, her face alive with pleasure. "If you count the babies. We have two foals, a filly called Dandelion and a colt called Chocolate Dream. He's called Mousse, because he's such a smoothie. Do you ride?"

"We've never had enough money.... Well, that's not true any longer, I guess," Sam floundered. "I can hardly wait to learn."

Bethany's warmth vanished and her momentarily open expression snapped shut like a steel trap.

"Mum runs a regular class for beginners," she said, not even trying to hide her scorn. "Tomorrow you can start in with all the other babies."

Sam did not respond. Bethany's mother frowned but let it pass.

"They're not babies," Josie said hotly. "My best friend Miles is in that class and so was Kenneth, until last year."

Kenneth said quietly but clearly enough for everyone in the car to hear, "Bethie is being mean because she has to share a room with you and she can't invite her friends for sleepovers. She was in the baby class herself two years ago. And she fell off Circus Rider last month."

"I didn't fall off," Bethany shouted, her cheeks going scarlet. "I got tossed off. It wasn't my fault. Circus Rider is hard to handle. Ask Mum."

"That's enough, kids. Why don't we all be quiet for a few moments and give Alex a chance to rest after her long journey?"

As she steered the car onto the highway, Mary Grantham switched on the cassette deck and a woman began to sing a song about being really mad.

Even Bethany laughed. They settled back to listen to Heather Bishop with appreciation. Sam, who had not heard her before, felt the tension inside her ease. Everything was going to be all right. She was going to meet fourteen horses. Beginner or not, she was going to ride.

Once on the highway, the trip was pretty uneventful, except that at one point they passed Alex and Mrs. Trueblood. Sam waved frantically but Alex seemed preoccupied. How strange that they should be driving in parallel lanes to different lives.

When they got to Guelph, Sam looked around with interest as they drove through the city, which seemed to have a lot of pretty, old stone buildings. As they were driving out of town, Mary Grantham pulled the car over in front of a narrow, old-fashioned store.

"I'll be right out," she said. "I have to pick up a book Mr. Trueblood got for me."

As Aunt Mary got out of the car, Sam glanced at the sign above the door and stiffened. READING MATTERS. Wasn't that the store Alex's people owned? She peered at it and read, in smaller letters, SECOND-HAND BOOKS BOUGHT AND SOLD. She thought furiously and was ready with a casual inquiry when Aunt Mary returned.

"How far is it from here to your place?" she asked.

"About four kilometres, I think. This is one of Josie and Kenneth's favourite places on earth. They're big readers like their father. Thomas loves to read, too, even though he's so young."

Kenneth nodded. "When I die," he said, "that's the place I'm going to haunt."

Aunt Mary laughed. Sam grinned. Bethany held

onto her scowl.

"That's sick," she muttered.

"They gave me the book you ordered too. I assume you'll reimburse me," his mother said, handing a fat volume to Kenneth.

The children began talking about horse books as the car picked up speed and headed out of the city.

Trying to break the ice, Sam pulled herself together and spoke directly to Bethany.

"What are the names of your other horses?" she asked.

Whether she got to ride them or not, she would at least hear their names. She loved the names of horses.

"Echo," Bethany began, sounding almost friendly. "Whistler. Beauregard. Pickwick. Dinah. Boomerang. Dilly. Frodo. Poppins. Moonbeam. Melody—she's my favourite."

Sam sat back. Bethany was off on a subject she loved. It would give Sam time to draw breath. It would allow her to get braced for whatever was coming next.

Suddenly she remembered Grandma's anxious face when they had said goodbye. If Grandma could see her now, she'd be shocked right out of her shoes!

Sam Scott choked back a whoop of laughter. Somehow she would have to get hold of herself or she would blow Alex's whole marvellous scheme.

She stared down at her hands and told herself that they belonged to someone called Alex. She had to get right inside the skin of Alexis Kennedy if she was going to make it work.

But the hands she clutched together remained the hands of Sam Scott.

6.

S am, put me out of my misery. Tell me right away
that you're an avid reader and a confirmed dog
lover," Mrs. Trueblood said, as she snapped the
buckle on her seat belt closed.

"I'm both," Alex told her. "I love reading better than
anything and I'm very fond of most dogs. How many do
you have?"

"Six when I left home," she said, smiling a little. "But
maybe more by now. Tiger, short for Tiger Lily, is away
becoming a father and Rosie has just been bred so we're
waiting to see if she is pregnant. I'm in a hurry to get back
because one of the bitches is whelping for the first time and
I'm anxious about her. My husband cares but he has the
shop to tend so he can't keep driving home to check on
Tansy. The people who bought Milkweed's last puppy

picked him up yesterday. Then there are Peony and Button—he's the papa of both Tansy's and Milkweed's pups."

The names sounded gentle but Alex pictured a pack of bull mastiffs or Great Danes and wondered if she should have stuck with the horses.

"What sort of dogs?" she asked, doing her best to sound relaxed.

"Papillons," Mrs. Trueblood replied. "They're tiny dogs, a toy breed. They're called 'papillons' because their big, upstanding ears make them look like butterflies. You know *papillon* is French for butterfly? I've had all sorts of dogs in my life, both as pets and to sell, but I like these the best. They're so … so … quick and funny and beautiful. Well, you'll see for yourself."

"I've never had a dog. Just a cat," Alex said. "He was Dad's. They had him destroyed."

"Who are 'they'?" Mrs. Trueblood asked, merging neatly with the traffic on the highway.

Alex pulled herself together, remembering almost too late that Sam had only her father. She thought fast.

"Dad and Grandma," she said lamely.

"How was your grandmother when you left?" asked Mrs. Trueblood.

Alex wasn't ready for this, but managed to say, "Fine. She saw me off at the airport."

"Well, let's hope the operation goes well. And how old was this cat of yours?"

"Nearly twenty," Alex said, searching for some way to change to a safer subject.

"Well, Sam, there's a time for all things under the sun," Mrs. Trueblood said quietly. "Your cat was probably ready to go. You were not ready to say goodbye but maybe he was. When you're that old and sick, life isn't much fun. Even I resent the twinges in my hinges and not hearing or seeing as well as I did five years ago."

Struggling not to look stunned at being called Sam, Alex said nothing. But she did take in what the old lady had said. She would think about it later, when she was alone and it would be safe to let her attention wander.

But there were no more awkward questions for the next ten minutes. The traffic was heavy and there was an accident in another lane. Trucks thundered past, blocking the view of road signs.

Then they reached a place where Mrs. Trueblood could pull off to the side for a moment.

"Let me call my husband and see how things are going," she said, picking up the car phone.

"Daniel, it is I," she said. "How's Tansy?"

When she hung up, she was much more relaxed.

"Nothing much is happening yet, Sam," she told Alex. "We may make it home in time if I step on the gas. Keep a weather eye out for policemen."

Because Alex had fixed her eyes on the highway, she saw the van containing the Grantham family and Sam pull slightly ahead of them. She stared after it, feeling lonelier and less lonely at one and the same moment. Already she had so much to tell Sam if and when they had a chance to compare notes that Sam would not get a word in for at least half an hour.

"How's your father?" her companion demanded suddenly.

"My father," Alex echoed. "You mean ..."

She almost said "my stepfather" but stopped herself in the nick of time.

"Dad's fine," she said lamely, her cheeks hot. "I just always call him Dad so I got muddled for a second."

Mrs. Trueblood smiled dryly.

"Father ... Dad ... I called mine Papa at first," she said. "I'm glad he's fine. I should have kept in closer touch with your grandmother but we're both busy women. If we aren't careful, we'll start settling for those disgusting non-letters people send at Christmas."

"What kind of letters?" Alex asked blankly.

"The kind you can send to a hundred people. They're newsletters, really, but they don't say a word about anything that really matters, your sorrows or your fears. They don't brag. They don't make jokes. They just tell, tell, tell. They're like pictures of houses from outside with the pretty wreath on the door. They are useful, I suppose, but all surface."

Alex gave her first relaxed grin. Perry had made Mum write one of those. She was mentioned but it wasn't really her at all: "Alex is doing well at school and is looking forward to moving into our new townhouse."

Mrs. Trueblood, who had been flying along and gaining on the Granthams' van, peered through the bug-spattered windshield and slowed down.

"There go the Granthams. You must have gotten to know that girl on the plane," she said, seeing Sam waving. "Mrs. Grantham and the oldest boy are two of our best customers. Bethany was, too, but she's preoccupied with puberty at the moment. Josie and I are fast friends although she finds sitting still a trial. Thomas was born to be a real reader. He pretends like mad. What's their visitor like?"

Alex was ready this time.

"I liked her," she said. "Look, Josie is waving at you."

"Hi, Josie," Mrs. Trueblood mouthed and waved back. "They live about a kilometre down our road. We're on the edge of town because we own more dogs than the city allows and they, of course, own horses. We do have neighbours without animals, but not many. Bethany rides past our front door often, exercising one or another of their steeds."

Alex stared at her. Was this good news or bad?

"Are they nice people?" she asked, doing her best to sound casual.

"Lovely," her hostess said absently.

Alex could tell the woman's thoughts were on Tansy. Now they were going way over the speed limit. They had swept through Guelph and zipped along the highway. Then, just as Alex was about to try to get her to slow down, they turned up a long drive running between arching shade trees to an old house. A dusty old car was parked in front. Mrs. Trueblood relaxed visibly, blowing out a long breath of relief.

"Daniel is with her," she said, and sprang out of the van, moving like a teenager. She must have been joking about her twinges. Alex, feeling shy, curious, and so nervous she felt sick to her stomach, followed in her wake. Dragging her suitcase behind, she was reminded of "Mary had a little lamb."

They charged right through the house into a part that had been built on at the back. Two tiny dogs came romping to meet them. They had enormous ears and plumy tails that were swirling and whirling with rapture at the return of their mistress.

A third stayed aloof from the others, sticking close to the woman wherever she went. "Yes, yes, hello," she said, wading through them to a half-open Dutch door. "Daniel, how is she?"

"She's had one beauty and now she's at work on number two. I think this'll be it. You must be Sam. Welcome to Windy Rise," the tall, stoop-shouldered man said, getting up from the chair where he had been keeping vigil.

"Thank you," Alex mumbled, looking over the half-door at Tansy.

The second puppy was in the process of diving out, headfirst. It appeared to be wrapped in a plastic sack. While Alex watched, the little dog broke the sack with her teeth and began to tidy up the tiny, squirming animal who had just arrived in the world.

"You can name this one, Sam, since you saw him born. I'm glad the first one is a girl. I'm going to call her Sweet Pea. Don't get too close. Newborn puppies can pick up an infection all too easily. We have to wash our hands before we go too near, and change our shoes. Daniel, could you show Sam her room?"

"Of course," the man said. "Then I must be off. Sean's at the shop. I called and asked him to come in early. But he'll get in a muddle if I don't get there soon."

"It *would* all happen on a Friday. Run along then. But thanks for babysitting," said Mrs. Trueblood, smiling at him and then heading for a nearby sink.

Alex's room was upstairs, looking out over a big property. The garden looked like a perfect place to explore. It was not all trim and neat with regular flower beds like those at the townhouse. The grass in the centre had been mowed but the rest was a wilderness of trees and shrubs. Mercury would have loved it when he was young enough to explore. The late afternoon sun was shedding a golden light over it all.

"You have the garden view. How's your father?" Daniel Trueblood asked suddenly.

"He's fine, as far as I know," Alex replied absent-mindedly. Then she remembered it was Sam's father they were discussing. "Very excited about this dig he's gone on," she added hurriedly.

"Good, good. Well, settle in and, when you're ready, go find my wife. She'll be hovering over Tansy."

Alex sat on the edge of the bouncy bed and listened to the man's retreating footsteps. Even when she heard the car pull away, she sat erect and wary. What had she and Sam done? Was it going to be all right? Could they keep up the pretense for as long as a day even and, if they couldn't, how would they explain themselves? She'd better start by claiming she was tired and going to bed early. In bed, she could think it all through.

Then, just as she thought she might explode, there was a scurry of small paws outside her door and two papillons came dancing in.

"They're Peony and Milkweed," Mrs. Trueblood's voice called from the foot of the stairs. "They wanted to check you out. All the dogs have flower names, some fancy, some weeds. Button is short for Bachelor's Button. He's growing old now. He's a one-woman dog. I'm afraid flower names for boys are a challenge. Come down when you please."

"Okay. Thanks," Alex called back.

Were there any flower names that would be perfect for a boy pup? Of course. Sweet William!

Alex smiled and Peony jumped onto her lap and put her paws up on her shoulders. She began washing her nose and cheeks with a tongue as delicate as a flower petal. Milkweed, who was much creamier, ran around the bed, sniffing the pillow and bedspread. Then she dashed over and biffed Peony with both paws. She flew off Alex's knee but bounced right back.

Alex laughed out loud. If only to meet these wonderful dogs, she was glad she and Sam had gone through with this crazy swap. She stroked the tall ears. They flattened under her hand and sprang up again. She thought she had never felt anything so soft.

"Hey, Milk and Pee, want to help me unpack?" she asked the two of them.

The tiny dogs looked at her and cocked their heads to listen. Their feathery tails swept in circles. Their whole bodies vibrated. Alex stood up and unzipped her bulging suitcase. Instantly Milkweed leapt in on top of the clean clothes and Peony sprang in on top of Milkweed.

It was a good thing Button was a one-woman dog!

Alex was helpless with laughter when Mrs. Trueblood called to her again. "Are they driving you nuts? Just say the word and I'll whistle them off."

"No, don't!" Alex cried. "They're great! How about Sweet William for the puppy?"

"Absolutely perfect! I can't think why I've never used it. I've had Bachelor's Button and a Jack-in-the-pulpit but no Sweet William," she called up.

At that moment, Alex realized, she felt utterly happy for the first time in weeks, not just happy on top but happy deep down inside. She hoped Sam was riding a marvellous horse and feeling just as joyous.

7

The Granthams' van had left the city of Guelph behind. Before long, it turned off down a country road, turned again, and pulled in. Sam stared wide-eyed at the cluster of buildings. There was a sign at the gate that read HERON HILL STABLES. Underneath a smaller one said something about riding lessons. Sam was on the wrong side of the car to read it. Anyway, she had no attention to spare. There stood a long, ramshackle house with toys on the wide front porch and lawn. Behind it was a weathered barn. Beyond that was another big building with its doors standing open. Sam saw it was a riding ring. She had never seen such a thing before except in old movies. And outside, across from the house, stretched a fenced field that had a ring with what she thought must be jumps. A man mounted on a tall black horse was out there talking to two boys on ponies. As the van stopped, the three riders dismounted and led their horses in a line toward the barn door.

Mary Grantham waved and told Sam that the man was her husband, Duncan.

"He took on a couple of my students so we could go meet the plane," she explained. "He has to go to Manitoba tomorrow to set up a computer system and do training with the staff. He'll be gone for a month or more. Horses don't pay enough to support this tribe of kids."

The Granthams and Sam trooped into the long sprawling house that was to be her home for the rest of the summer—if she didn't wreck everything before bedtime and get shipped out. She could not be sent back to British Columbia, of course, since Dad was already somewhere in South America, too far for Sam to follow, and Grandma would be checking into the hospital tomorrow morning. But she'd be dumped off at the bookstore, for certain. Would these people be understanding and take Alex in exchange? She was not sure why, but she had her doubts.

"Here we are, Alex," Mary Grantham said, leading the way into a big kitchen. "Your home away from home for a while."

There was a small waiting silence. Sam looked at the woman's expectant face and did her best to be a credit to Grandma.

"It's really good of you to have me," she said, struggling not to let her voice wobble.

"Well, we have quite a full house but I'm glad to help where I can," came the answer.

Sam ached to rush out of the house and go see the horses but she made herself stand still and keep quiet.

Mary Grantham strode over to a wall phone and pushed a button to hear her messages. Kenneth headed into a side room where Sam soon heard a TV being turned on.

Then a small boy, who looked about five, came trundling into the kitchen to stare at her. His dark hair hung down over his big brown eyes. He had rosy cheeks, and Sam, who had not had much experience with young children, wanted to pick him up and hug him. He had on a pair of short shorts, a Superman cape, and red rubber boots. He did not smile but studied her solemnly.

"Are you Alice?" Thomas Grantham asked.

Sam stared back at him, wondering what on earth he meant.

"No, dumdum. She's not Alice. She's Alex," Bethany said. "Say Alex. You can't go around calling her Alice."

Thomas ignored his sister entirely.

"Hi, Alice," he said. "Tom likes you. You be my fwend?"

This time, Sam needed no interpreter. She squatted down in front of him.

"Sure, I'll be your friend," she told him. "And you can call me Alice if you can't say Alex."

"Can say it. Not want to," Thomas told her with a big grin. Then he was off, trotting after the others.

"He's sweet," Sam said. Then, catching the forlorn look on Josie's face, she added quickly, "Nobody has ever called me Alice before."

Nobody had called her Alex either. She must remember to answer when they did. It was not going to be easy.

"Sweet as a dose of poison ivy," Bethany muttered. "Can I go, Mum?"

"No, Bethany, you may not. Take Alex up and show her where she's to sleep. Then, before you go near a horse, you'll have some supper, if only a sandwich. Alex, you need to freshen up after your trip. Your hair could do with a brush and your shirt has chocolate right down the front. A horse might take you for a tasty snack. I'll have something ready for you both to eat when you come down. Afterwards, you can take Alex on the Grand Tour of Heron Hill Stables."

She smiled broadly at Sam and turned away as though she had not just told her she looked a mess. Bethany flushed slightly and gave her mother's back a dirty look. Then she turned to stalk out of the kitchen. Sam followed meekly, lugging her duffle bag. Bethany turned left, climbed a long staircase, and went down a hall, passing one door that stood open. The older girl glanced in at the chaos and groaned.

"Thomas has been in there," she explained. "We have safety hooks on our doors to keep him out but we must have forgotten this one. He loves pushing buttons, drawing on walls, and dumping out bottles of whatever he can find. I'm warning you, Alex. If you value your belongings, never leave them where he can get at them. Keep coming." Sam had paused to listen. The impatience in Bethany's voice started her moving again.

The room they were to share was large and sunny. It had twin beds, twin dressers, posters of beautiful horses galloping, and a big bookcase. One shelf held books. The rest displayed a collection of statues of horses. There were wooden carvings of them, ceramic ones, a glass one, and some plastic ones. They were all different shades. There was even a blue one made of porcelain.

"Wow," Sam said, awestruck. She dropped her bag and crossed the room to look at each one. "They're great! Some are so beautiful! Those are lovely."

She pointed to a row of six wooden horses, hand-carved and special-looking, walking in a line on the highest shelf.

Bethany did not answer for a second. Then she said, in a softened voice, "I've been collecting them since I was seven. My godmother in Taiwan sent me those. They're Chinese. I have stuffed ones, too. Look."

Sam turned and saw four more horses on one of the beds. One was a Beanie Baby. One was made of patchwork. One was knitted. It didn't look like a horse exactly but it didn't look like any other animal. It had a mane and tail but its head was round and it had blue eyes. The last horse was smaller and very worn. Bethany picked it up and stroked its nose with one finger. Her smile was tender as well as self-mocking.

"This was the first," she said. "Her name is Queen of the Wind. I thought she was perfect."

"I think she's neat," Sam said, liking Bethany better for a moment. "She looks so knowing."

"Yeah," the other girl said, putting her horse down again gently. "I guess she is. I told her all my secrets for months and for years I held onto her when I went to sleep."

"I have something like that," Sam mumbled, stooping to unzip her bag. "I thought I might not get him out but I couldn't leave him behind in Vancouver. He was my mother's when she was small."

She dug through the clothes until she felt Lamb. He was curly and black and beguiling although obviously worn by years of being hugged, rolled on, dropped, kissed, and loved enthusiastically.

"He's cute," Bethany said, glancing at him and looking away. She did smile, but it was not the smile she would have given if Lamb had been a horse, Sam thought. She also looked as though she had not meant to confide in the interloper Sam knew herself to be. No warmth was left in the older girl's face as she explained how much space was allotted to Sam.

"I bet you have your own room at home, don't you, Alex?" she said.

"Yes," Sam said after a split second. How long would it take for her to know "Alex" meant her? "I'm an only child. There's no one to share with."

"It must be wonderful," Bethany sighed, tossing her head and rolling her eyes. "Sometimes I feel as though I have to share the air I breathe and there isn't enough to go around. Mum says we're lucky to be part of a large family, but she only had one sister and they always had their own rooms so what does she know?"

"I've always wished for a sister," Sam said after another slight pause. She turned her head so the other girl could not look into her face and spoke in a low voice, not wanting Bethany to guess how lonely she had often felt with just her father and grandmother for family.

"I sure would not want a stepfather. My real father is great when he has spare time, but not when he's working with computers. He travels a lot. What's your stepfather like?"

Sam had no idea what to say. She looked at the floor and bit her lip, trying desperately to remember what Alex had let fall about Perry. She did not like him much, she was pretty sure. Would it be safe to make a face and leave it at that?

"Never mind if it makes you feel awful," Bethany burst out hurriedly, sitting down and staring at Sam's bent head. "I mean … is he cruel to you?"

Her lips had parted and her eyes were greedy for details. She looked like the older sisters of Sam's friends when they were whispering secrets not to be overheard by younger children. Sam was glad, all at once, that she knew nothing evil about Alex's stepfather. Bethany might have pried it out of her and she would have ended up feeling like a traitor.

"Not cruel," Sam said. "I think step-parents get a bad rap. I have a friend who likes her stepmother better than her birth mother. Maybe Perry will grow on me. He hasn't been around all that long."

That should be safe, she thought.

"Well, your own father took off and left you, didn't he? That was cruel," Bethany said definitely. "You must hate him. My dad would never do that."

"Hate my father?" Sam echoed blankly. She thought of her dad, who was the person she loved best in the whole world, even though he was a bit vague and too bookish. She could not hate him if she tried.

Then, in the nick of time, she realized Bethany did not mean her father but Alex's. All the same, she was positive that Alex, too, cared about her real father. Her dad had left her that cat she had spoken about.

"My father left me his cat," she said. "Mercury. Mum had him put to sleep. But Dad gave him to me before he went away—and going wasn't his idea. Mum told him he'd have to leave if he couldn't get a proper job."

"Oh," Bethany said, losing interest. "I'm not a cat person, I guess. I don't trust them. They kill birds."

"You eaten any chicken lately?" Sam asked, knowing she was not being fair but not caring. She had never laid eyes on Alex's old cat but she was not going to let this cold-hearted girl insult him.

"Girls, your food is ready," Mary Grantham called before Bethany could retort. "Get washed and come on down."

Sam sighed with relief. She had been rescued before she gave the whole show away.

"Don't forget to put on a clean shirt," Bethany said sweetly, when Sam swung around to start through the door. "And brush your hair. I know your hair is short but it's all on end. My mother is a neat freak."

Sam yearned to punch her or say something really cutting but she could not think of anything nasty enough, and anyway she felt too tense. Keeping a grip on her temper, she pulled a comb through her crisp curls and yanked a clean T-shirt over her head. She would call Alex first chance she got. They would have to confess. She could not stand living with this family another day.

Then she remembered the horses.

It was too late for riding now, she thought, but at least she could meet them. Okay. She would keep still until she saw the horses. Then she was out of here.

After Alex had unpacked her stuff and put her clothes away in the chest of drawers Mrs. Trueblood had said she could use, she stayed upstairs and played with Peony and Milkweed for a while. But delightful as they were, she grew restless after half an hour and it was still early evening. She could not settle down with a book, not after having sat still all those hours on the plane. She needed to explore.

With the tiny dogs dancing ahead of her, she went down to the kitchen and found her hostess starting to get supper.

"Can I help?" Alex asked politely, hoping the woman would say no.

"No need. You go out and get some fresh air. The dogs can go along. You all need to stretch your legs."

Alex peered out the kitchen window. There was a long strip of lawn with bushes all around the edge. Mrs. Trueblood clearly liked roses, for there were several kinds and they were all lovely. Alex saw, on the other side of some lilac bushes, a stone cottage. The little house looked asleep.

"Who lives next door?" she asked.

"His name is George Carr. He's a widower in his eighties. His wife died in March and he's turned himself into a recluse since he lost her. He has Parkinson's, which slows him down some, but he's still very independent. It would be nice if you could make friends with him while you're here."

Alex kept her face blank and looked at the pattern of tiles on the kitchen floor. Why on earth would she make friends with a sick old man who didn't like people? She didn't know any old men. Mum's father had died when Alex was too young to remember him, and Dad's father had died before she was born. The very thought of trying to befriend a sick man who was over eighty made her want to run away.

"Why don't you go and introduce yourself?" said Mrs. Trueblood, as if she were suggesting a treat. "I think he's out in his garden now. He worries me. I heard him come out when I was taking the peelings to the compost. Run along, Sam, and say hello."

Alex was startled. In Vancouver, she would never be sent out alone that way to introduce herself to some stranger. It was just next door, of course, but in her life at home some adult was always watching over her. She was not allowed to go exploring the way Dad had encouraged her to do when they lived in Victoria.

They had moved to Vancouver when she was five so that her mother could go to work in an office devoted to investing people's money. For her mother, Vancouver was a city filled with lurking dangers, waiting to pounce on her only child. The anxiety had eased after Perry came along, but only because her mother was distracted.

"Is it okay for me to go out on my own?" she asked shyly.

"Of course," Mrs. Trueblood said briskly, going on chopping vegetables. "You can't get into trouble in our backyard. Besides, I feel sure you are a sensible girl, able to look out for yourself."

Alex laughed delightedly and went to the back door. It opened on the lawn she had glimpsed through the window. It was not a tidy, smooth, bright green one but raggedy, with daisies growing in the grass and big bushes hanging over it at the edges. Behind the bushes was a neat fence with no holes through which small dogs could escape. But, at the far end, there was a gate. Alex strolled down the length of the garden and peered over the gate.

As she did, she heard a crash and a yelp. What was that?

Then she saw the old man. He had toppled over backwards into a rose bush. His feet were off the ground so he could not right himself. Also, the thorny branches had snagged his shirt and scratched him. Blood was oozing from his forehead and his cheek was scraped. His face was a strange colour. It looked as though he had been flushed but now the flush had drained away, leaving him grey.

Alex stood frozen, paralyzed with shock.

"Help," moaned the old man in a quavering voice. "Can anybody hear me? I'm stuck in this bloody bush. Help!"

Alex swung open the gate and ran to him. She was still not sure what to do. The man glared up at her but he did not seem to be seeing her clearly. It was as though he were looking at her through a misted window. His eyes squinched up under their bushy white brows.

"Is someone there?" he asked. "If you are, speak up and stop hovering."

Then Alex spotted his glasses lying on the grass. She picked them up, amazed they were not broken. Leaning over, she placed them on his nose, hooking the side pieces over his ears. At once, his vague, disjointed face seemed to snap together. He could see her now. His eyes drilled into her face. Yet they were frightened eyes. He must wonder who she was.

"Did you fall?" she asked him.

"No!" he barked. "I always take an afternoon nap in this rose bush. Of course I fell. Help me up, girl."

He was wheezing and now his face was turning red in patches.

Alex stepped closer, reached out her hands, and tried to pull him up by his elbows. Her damp palms slipped on his bony arms and he grunted in pain.

"I'll go get help," she said, her voice shaking as much as his had done.

"No. You can do it, girl. If the others come, they'll be carting me off in an ambulance before you can say a word. I hate fuss and I'm sure nothing is broken. Take my two hands in yours and brace your feet. Now lean back. I don't weigh all that much. Just a bundle of old bones in a wrinkled skin sack."

Alex was afraid of dropping him again and really hurting him but something in the way his eyes were fixed on her face kept her from fetching Mrs. T., much as she longed to. She swallowed. Then she stretched out her hands and grasped his. They were thin with knobbly joints. Band-Aids were stuck on two of his fingers, but they were strong and hard.

The rose bush did not want to release him but he held onto her with a bruising grip and slowly but surely she hauled him out of it.

"Don't let me go," he gasped as he came upright.

"I won't," Alex gasped back, holding on for dear life as they swayed off balance in a weird sort of dance. He caught his breath at last and muttered, "Just wait until I've got my pins under me."

He was clutching her so she could not have let go if she had wanted to. His grip was like iron. Her slim fingers felt crushed but she tried not to let the pain show on her face. Then he shifted one hand to her shoulder and straightened up, bearing his own weight.

"It's my balance," he told her, wheezing. "I have Parkinson's disease and it makes me wobbly. Who are you, anyway, and where did you spring from?"

She remembered her new name just in time.

"I'm Sam Scott," she said. "I'm staying with the Truebloods for the summer."

"Oh, yes," he mumbled. "I remember. Just walk me as far as the back door. You're a good child to take so much trouble over me."

Then they were at the back entry of the cottage. She was about to come in with him but he brushed her aside.

"I'll be right as rain now," he said. "This little tumble is our secret, yours and mine. If my nephew heard, it would give him just the excuse he's been looking for to clap me into some nursing home. He wants to put me away so he can stop 'worrying,' but I want no part of his dratted Sunset Haven. Worry won't kill him. You run along now, Sam, and remember to keep mum."

He closed the door with a bang and she could hear him shuffling away. She also heard somebody speak. Or she thought she did. She wondered if she had dreamed it, though, because the voice seemed to say, "Please put a penny in the old man's hat." Hadn't Mrs. Trueblood said he lived alone?

She started to run and tell Mrs. Trueblood all about it but then slowed down.

"Our secret," he had said. "Keep mum."

She had not heard that expression before but she understood its meaning. No telling Mrs. Trueblood. Wait till she told Sam, though. Telling Sam wouldn't count. If only she and Sam could get a chance to talk privately.

Neither Alex nor Sam felt at home as they had supper that evening. Sam had a sandwich and a bowl of ice cream. She could tell right away that, although her hostess liked eating, cooking was not Mary Grantham's main interest in life any more than it was Bethany's. Feeling tired and far from home, she chewed each bite and swallowed it down without tasting it.

She was still excited about the horses, but even so, she did not want to keep up the pretending for the whole summer. She would have to get Alex to agree to tell all after a couple of days, however hard it would be.

Alex had stew. She loathed stew. Mrs. Trueblood had made a big salad and there was lots of bread so Alex did her best to hide the stew under her cutlery and fill up on salad and bread and cheese.

"I despised stew when I was your age," Mrs. Trueblood said calmly. "I should have ordered pizza. Why don't you call me Margaret? Mrs. Trueblood is an awful mouthful. Your mother called me Godma when she was small but I'm not your godmother or your aunt."

Alex stared down at her plate and blushed. She could not imagine calling this old lady Margaret even though she had changed into jeans and a sweatshirt before supper. The shirt had writing on it. "I have nothing to declare but my genius." Alex had grinned when she puzzled it out. It was something Oscar Wilde had said, whoever he was. Then she remembered his name. He was the author of one of her favourite stories, "The Happy Prince." She had cried buckets over it when her father had read it to her.

"All right ... Margaret," she got out in a very small voice.

Mrs. Trueblood laughed.

"You'll soon get used to it. Josie Grantham calls me Margaret without a thought. Thomas calls me Mrs. Bloody but that's Thomas. I won't be Mrs. Bloody for anyone else."

Alex laughed and felt much better all at once.

That night, she lay in her strange bed in the room that had been made ready for Sam. She felt very alone. She did not want her mother or Perry but she missed her very own pillow with the pillowcase her father had sent her for Christmas. It had a picture of a cow stuck halfway while trying to jump over the moon and it read "Nothing is ever simple." Having it under her cheek was like having Dad with her, understanding everything. And it was so true that nothing was ever simple.

She wanted Merc too, even though she was used to being without him now. Then she felt two small scrambles and thumps. Milkweed and Peony leapt up onto the bed and licked her nose and cheeks with the softest tongues in the world and then prowled around until they chose their sleeping spots.

"Aww, you're adorable," she breathed, reaching to stroke the magic silky ears.

Their tails swished in delighted response. Then they sighed contentedly and settled themselves, one at her back and one under her chin.

"Shall I remove them?" Margaret asked from the doorway. "They've taken a shine to you but if you can't stand having them …"

"No. I love having them," Alex told her.

She was no longer one bit lonely.

"They know how to console," Margaret said as she turned away, "and they like a girl who goes to bed earlier than we do."

Alex smiled at this but her thoughts had gone to her partner in crime.

"How are you doing, Sam?" she whispered into the darkness. "Have you got a horse to cuddle?"

Sam should have felt less alone than Alex since she had Bethany to keep her company. But she was used to having a room to herself. She was afraid to make any noise. She lay struggling to relax, hugging her black lamb tightly. She wished morning would come so she could phone Alex and plan how to get out of the mess they were in.

She turned onto her stomach at last. She felt like crying even though she hardly ever wept over things. Also, she was positive Bethany was lying there, wide awake, ears cocked for the first sniffle. Sam Scott was not about to give her the satisfaction.

The Grand Tour had been a crashing disappointment. Just as they stepped outside, it had begun to rain.

"You can see it all from here," Bethany had said. "The horses are asleep by now. Dad and Ken took care of them with those kids to help. You can see the riding ring. You saw it from the car. Oh, I'm tired. I'm sorry if you're horse-crazy but I'm not in the mood. And Mum said to get to bed early since you must be jet-lagged."

Sam had stared at her in astonishment. Bethany was obviously in one heck of a bad mood.

"Whatever you say," she said.

"You better believe it," the other girl growled, and ran to the TV set. She clearly had a favourite program she wanted to watch. Sam trailed after her. It was one she personally thought infantile even though it was intended for teenagers.

She sat down and shut her eyes so she would look worn out. Finally Mary Grantham noticed and ordered them up to bed. Bethany stomped her feet on every step and barely spoke once they reached the bedroom.

Somewhere downstairs a clock chimed. She counted the bongs. It was only eleven. She had hours to lie there staring into the dark. But she *was* jet-lagged and after she heard Bethany give a gentle snore, she slept.

*A*fter breakfast, Alex went outside to see if Mr. Carr was back in the rose bush. He was sitting in his lawn chair instead. He looked at her over his spectacles. He did not smile. But she knew somehow he was glad she was there.

"Good day, young woman," he said. "Come on through the gate if you must."

It wasn't exactly a warm welcome but she did as she was told.

"Help yourself to a cookie," he said gruffly, pushing a tin toward her. It held, among others, her favourite kind, shortbread cookies, and she beamed at him as she took two and dropped to sit next to him on the grass. She was munching happily and basking in the morning sunlight falling through the leaves on his tall locust tree when he took her off guard.

"What's your name again?" he shot at her.

"Alex," she said automatically and then, too late, clapped her hand over her mouth, spraying cookie crumbs in all directions.

He stared at her, his eyes puzzled. Shocked to the core, she stared back. Her thoughts were stuttering in helpless confusion.

"I thought you said ... Well, never mind. Short for Alexandra, I suppose?" he inquired mildly.

"Alexis," Alex told him. She did not know what else to do.

Oh, Sam, I'm sorry, wailed a voice inside her head. I didn't mean to. It just popped out.

"What's come over you, child?" the old man asked sharply. "There's nothing wrong with your name. Why are you looking as though you'd been hit by lightning?"

"It's just that I'm going by the name of Sam right now," Alex tried to explain but found herself hopelessly lost. "It's a secret, a sort of disguise. We started it on the plane ..."

She petered out.

"'We'! Who is this 'we'?" he shot at her.

Then the whole story came pouring out in disjointed half-sentences. He mustn't tell, she begged him.

After listening for a while, Mr. Carr hoisted himself up from his chair.

"I think we'd better continue this discussion indoors," he said. "We don't want eavesdroppers. And you're beginning to mumble. Come on. Give me your arm. I'm still creaky from my tumble into the rose bush."

As they entered the kitchen, she heard voices down in the basement. She jumped.

"Who's that?" she demanded in a fierce whisper.

"It must be the radio," he said, sounding testy.

He went ahead of her to a living room and a big armchair that waited for him in front of a fireplace. He sank into the chair, glancing over at the door that led to the basement stairs.

"Close that, would you?" he said, breathing hard.

"I could go down and switch it off," Alex ventured.

"No," he snapped. "Shut the door and get back here. I'm waiting to hear about this name change of yours."

Confused and hurt, Alex went over and did as he had told her.

She had betrayed Sam and made Mr. Carr mad. A weight of guilt settled on her shoulders as he struggled to catch his breath.

Then he grinned up at her downcast face.

"Begin at the beginning and tell all," he ordered.

Alex was astonished to find herself smiling back. Maybe it was funny after all. Maybe Sam would laugh too.

Mr. Carr's deep chuckle lifted the heaviness off her spirit

as if the burden were nothing but feathers. Suddenly, she was sure that Sam would understand.

When Sam awoke, nothing looked quite so bad. Maybe she should wait another couple of days before confessing. At least she would get to ride a horse first.

They were in the middle of breakfast when Bethany asked Sam the name of the other girl who had been on the plane with her.

"How would she know?" their mother began.

Sam took a chance.

"I do know," she said, as casually as she could. "We sat together. Her name's Sam. She's visiting the people who run that bookstore."

"I wondered if that was who she was," Kenneth said. "We know the Truebloods, and Mrs. T. said they had a girl coming. They live just up the road."

Sam's heart leapt with delight but she managed to keep her face more or less blank.

"What's Mrs. Trueblood like?" she asked, and bit into her piece of toast.

"She's frumpy," Bethany said.

"She is not," Josie said hotly. "She's the nicest grown-up we know. She calls me 'Honeybunch.'"

"I didn't say 'grumpy.' Her clothes are frumpy. Hurry up,

Alex. I've got to get out to the stable," Bethany said, ignoring her little sister's sulky glare completely.

Sam was irritated but she, too, wanted to go to the stable so she began to gobble the berries she had been given. Bethany snatched up the bowl the moment Sam spooned the last bite into her mouth and shoved both their bowls into the dishwasher. Then she led Sam out through the back door. Kenneth, book in hand, melted away but Josie tagged after them. Bethany strode across the big yard to the stable. She swung the door open and a dozen or more horses' heads poked out of a line of stalls.

"This one's my pet," Bethany said, producing a couple of sugar cubes and holding them out on her flattened palm to a gigantic glossy black horse with a white star on his forehead. "You are my beautiful boy, aren't you, Beauregard?"

The tall horse leaned down and took the sugar as daintily as a lady in a jewellery shop picks up a diamond. His large ears tipped forward, listening to every word Bethany uttered. He was gorgeous. But so very big!

Sam had seen horses through car windows and in movies but she had never stood this close to a real live one. She had expected to look up to them but not to have to crane her neck.

The smell of the horses was astonishing too. She breathed it in. It made the moment real. Horses in books never smelled like this.

Beau whinnied. It sounded like the trumpeting of an elephant, and Sam nearly jumped out of her skin.

"He's Dad's horse, not hers," Josie muttered.

Before Sam had recovered from this startling bit of information, Bethany had pushed past her and begun to saddle up a dark brown horse, not quite as tall as Beau but still huge.

"Her name is Melody," she said over her shoulder, grunting as she heaved the saddle over the horse's back, and, before Sam could comment, she had the horse out of her stall. She led Melody from the stable into the riding ring with Sam and Josie tagging along. Sam watched wide-eyed as the other girl swung up onto the mare's back and rode her down the track that ran around the big circular space. Sam felt green with envy and angry at being more or less ignored. She also felt scared.

"Can I ride?" she burst out as Bethany pulled up in front of her and waited for some sort of comment. Sam was not at all sure she herself wanted to ride any longer but she had to get the suspense over with. If she could not manage, she had better find out fast.

The other girl looked down at her with a glint in her eyes that promised something unpleasant. The spite was hidden away in an instant but Sam had seen. She braced herself for whatever was coming. Bethany dismounted nimbly and looped Melody's reins around a post.

"Of course you can," she said—too sweetly. "I'll saddle

up Dinah. She's patient and used to people who don't really know how to ride."

Sam stiffened. She also felt her cheeks grow hot. But she managed to keep her anger squashed down. Bethany wanted to make her feel dumb. She probably would make her look dumb too. Well, too bad about Bethany. Sam just wanted a chance to ride. She might not disgrace herself. She might be a born rider for all anyone knew.

"Whatever you say," she said coolly.

She waited for Bethany to carry out her little plot.

Bethany did not look at Sam while she hoisted a saddle onto the broad back of an old dun-coloured mare with a ragged black mane.

Sam studied her and decided Dinah did not look fierce or tricky. She looked bored out of her mind.

"Mum said Alex should ride Echo," Josie piped up, glaring at her sister.

"We have to find out if she can handle herself on horseback first," Bethany said smoothly, not looking at either of the other girls. "There you go, Alex."

Sam was glad she had just watched the other girl mount or she would have started with the wrong foot. As it was, she felt incredibly awkward. But she managed to swing up and felt as though she were doing the splits. She also felt far too high up. Her insides wobbled like jelly that had not yet set properly.

"Yikes!" she shrieked inside her head.

Although Sam kept her voice almost steady when she told the horse to move, Dinah didn't trot or canter or even walk with any spirit. She plodded along, taking lots of time to think things over. She bent her head and sniffed the ground as though she were searching for a snack of fresh buttercups.

"Don't let her get away with that," Bethany called, her voice scornful. She had remounted Melody and was trotting briskly past. "Dig your toes into her ribs and keep her head up."

Bethany reached out as she went by and whacked Dinah's rump with a switch she held in her hand. Startled, the old horse actually went into an uneven trot. Now Sam was jouncing up and down like a sack of potatoes. She opened her mouth and almost bit through her tongue as she came down hard again. Then she managed to swallow the shriek before it escaped. What had ever made her long to do this? It was pure punishment.

If it had lasted, Sam might have slid off, but Dinah, sensing she was safe, soon slowed down again. Sam tried to speed her up but Dinah was not to be hurried along by a gentle nudge. She completely ignored all her inexperienced rider's attempts to get her moving.

Then Aunt Mary and Kenneth came out.

"Oh, Bethany, why didn't you get Alex a decent horse?" the woman called, sounding very annoyed. "I told you to put her up on Echo. Dinah is so stubborn and lazy. Dismount,

Alex, and we'll saddle another horse for you. And where's your riding helmet?"

Sam made no reply. For the first time, she saw that Bethany had pulled on a helmet, although the strap was not fastened. She must have jammed it on when she saw Aunt Mary coming. Had it been hanging on the saddle? Sam thought it might have been.

She was proud of herself as she dismounted without landing upside-down but she shook her head at the offer of Echo even though she liked the look of her. She was a creamy, dappled horse with a gentle expression. She, too, was big but Sam was getting used to horses being big.

Once she reached the ground, however, Sam kept her face blank and her eyes lowered. She would ride again but not right now. She felt a cold ball of resentment growing inside her like a snowball rolling downhill. She had read lots of books about horses. Dad wanted her to read other kinds of books but she liked horse books best. And, in the stories, the best horses would sense how tense the rider was. It would spoil the ride for them both.

She thought of Flicka, Ken MacLaughlin's filly in the one horse book her father had given her for her tenth birthday. It was called *My Friend Flicka* and it was her favourite. It was a real book, not a pony club book written for babies. Echo was as smart as Flicka; she would guess Sam was not in a riding mood.

"I'd rather wait until later," she managed to say calmly.

"Bethany, I'm ashamed of you," Aunt Mary was beginning when Sam, with Kenneth at her side and Josie tagging along, moved off. Other children were arriving for lessons so Bethany and her mother were too busy to attend to Sam's problems.

10

ow about doing something non-equine?"
Kenneth said, glancing at Sam's stiff
face.

"What's 'non-equine' mean?" Josie demanded.

Sam laughed.

"Equine means horse," she told the little girl. "I'd love
to do something non-equine for a while. What did you
have in mind?"

Thomas came trotting up to them.

"Want to see the river?" he asked without a hint of baby
talk.

"Sounds perfect," Sam told him, fascinated by the
change in his speech. "How come you sound so much
older?"

Thomas's eyes sparkled but he did not answer.

"He sucks up to Mum. He's her sweet baby boy," Josie said, scornfully. "Grown-ups think he's adorable."

"I *am* adorable," Thomas said smugly.

"Our river is really just a stream," Kenneth explained as they all trooped after the small boy. "I guess it looks bigger when you're little. But it's nice and you should know where it is in case you want to go wading."

"My grandmother calls it 'paddling,'" Sam said. "She's English."

She could have bitten her tongue as she saw a surprised look in Kenneth's eyes.

"I thought Mum said you only had a mother and a step-father," he said.

"I meant before she died," Sam said, hoping against hope she was not getting in deeper. Talking about Alex's family was like going wading in water on a bed of sand that suddenly dropped away and left you floundering out of your depth.

"Both our grandmothers are American," Kenneth said, not sounding at all suspicious. "We haven't seen them since just after Thomas was born. One is in Texas and the other lives in a special village where only old people live. It's called Cozy Corners."

Sam gaped at him.

"It's really true," he told her, laughing out loud at her disgusted look. "It sounds awful, doesn't it?"

"Here we are," Thomas said. "Sit here, Alice. It's the best sitting rock."

It was lovely. The stream was deep in the middle but shallow at the edge. Before long, they had all taken off their shoes. As they looked at the darting minnows and studied a small green frog Ken had caught, Sam stopped wanting to punch out Bethany. She even stopped wanting to leave. Gruesome Bethany was only one kid, after all. The other three were great.

When she looked around for her left running shoe, Thomas had it balanced on one hand above his head. He laughed and tossed it to her. His aim was poor and she had to scramble after it.

"How do you spell Alice?" his voice called.

She looked back at him. He was studying her with a funny look in his eyes.

"A-L-E-X," she said, "if you mean my name."

"I thought so," Thomas said, and he ran off, laughing.

They went back to the house for lunch and afterwards Sam finally got her chance to ride properly.

"This is Echo," Aunt Mary said, introducing Sam to the cream-coloured horse whose coat was dappled and whose face was long and gentle. The horse gazed down at Sam as though she were deciding what she thought of her.

"Wow, she's wonderful," Sam breathed, stroking the bony nose. It was hard and yet warmly alive. Between Echo's eyes, there was a swirl of hair which, Aunt Mary said, identified her like a fingerprint.

"Here, Alex," Josie said, grinning wickedly as she handed Sam some chunks of raw carrot and two sugar cubes. They had all been in the pocket of her shorts and lint clung to them but Sam knew the horse would not care. She flattened her palm and extended her hand with a large piece of carrot on it. That was how Ken gave Flicka treats.

Echo's rubbery lips surrounded the offering and then the carrot was gone. Sam swallowed and slowly pulled her hand back to safety, not making any false moves. Alex had been right about horses having humongous teeth. Yet she was not really scared now, and by the time she held out the last of the sugar, she felt like an experienced horsewoman. She grinned up at Echo's big eye looking down at her. It was beautiful and it was communicating two messages clearly: "I like you, strange girl," and "Bring more food next time."

"Well, let's saddle them up and give them a little exercise," Bethany said casually. "We'll see if she's as sweet-tempered as she is pretty. Here's a bridle and saddle you can use."

"And a helmet," Josie murmured, stretching up to pluck one off a hook.

Sam's knees quivered. Thank goodness her jeans hid the tremble. She smiled her thanks at Josie, though, and put on the riding helmet first. She had never saddled up a horse in her entire life. Maybe, if she did exactly what Bethany did, she could manage. Step one: pull the thing up over the long nose …

She fell behind in less than a minute. Bethany had been saddling horses for years. Sam had no idea why parts of the saddle were so hard to handle. She dropped it twice and felt as though every finger on both her hands had become a numb thumb.

"Let me, Alex. You'll never be ready that way. It takes practice," Aunt Mary told her.

Humbly, Sam stood back and watched her do the difficult job deftly, not wasting a motion or fumbling once. Would Sam get that good in time? Never.

"Come on," Bethany called. "Lead her out here and mount up."

Sam, positive Echo would not move an inch for her, took up the rein and stepped out the door. Clop, clop, cloppity. Echo followed along as good as gold. She blew a great, gusty warm breath on the back of Sam's neck. It tickled and it felt magical.

Bethany mounted so swiftly that Sam felt humiliated again. Was the other girl showing off on purpose or just being her normal self? A bit of both?

Sam gritted her teeth, held her breath, and did what she had seen Bethany do that morning. Then she, Samantha Cecily Scott, was sitting astride a mile-high horse. Echo, sensing her nervousness, stirred but settled down after a minute. Bethany shot the pair of them a scornful glance.

"Giddy-up," she told Melody. Her horse gave a small prance and began to move in a brisk walk. Right behind her came Sam on Echo. Even though they were moving slowly, she jounced up and down. It hurt. Whump, bump, wham!

She was sure she looked as totally awkward as she felt. The bones in her bottom hit the saddle and were thrown up, only to land just as hard the next moment. She could not seem to prevent a single jarring thud. She looked at Bethany's knees and saw that they were stiffened somehow. She did her best to copy the other girl's posture and found herself landing a little more gently. Even if she was doing it all wrong, she didn't care. Her dream was coming true. Terrified though she still was, she was riding a horse and Echo was great.

Then Bethany set Melody trotting. Echo followed suit. Sam clung on like a burr for one minute. Then one of her feet slipped out of its stirrup. Sam knew that before Bethany was finished with her, she was going to plummet off and disgrace the name of Scott ... or Kennedy.

But she gritted her teeth and forced her foot back into the swinging stirrup. She pulled back on the rein. Echo seemed to understand. She slowed to a comforting walk again.

"I won't fall off," Sam told herself. "I will not. I will not!"

She felt strangely calm, as though she were casting a spell over herself and Echo both. Then, to her own astonishment, she and her horse moved smoothly forward into a canter. She just let herself relax into it. A breath of wind came across the fields and ran cool fingers over her hot cheeks. And she filled up and brimmed over with a power she had never felt before. For a second, she flew. This was why people loved their horses. "Good going, Alex," Josie cheered from her perch on the fence.

"Why don't you try galloping now?" Bethany called.

"Not today," Sam called back over her shoulder. She was panting and a knife thrust of panic was slicing through her calm. Echo slowed to a trot, and once more Sam felt all the bones and joints in her back and hips getting bruised. Her knees, struggling to grip the horse's sides, would not tighten properly. They were used to sitting on a chair, not straddling a tall mare. But Bethany's taunting words no longer had the power they had had an hour before.

She loosened her knees and slouched in the saddle. Echo slowed to a saunter. Bethany went cantering by, her ponytail flipping up and down. She and her horse moved together, as smoothly as if they were one creature instead of two, just the way the horse books said they should.

Sam stared after them, wide-eyed with admiration. Well, she would learn, she thought, as she wiped the back of one hand across her sweaty face. Bethany's pace looked far too dangerous. Sam made up her mind to go on watching until she grew accustomed to being so far above the ground.

When she had been riding without anything dire happening for another half-hour, Aunt Mary's sensible voice broke in on the exciting new experience.

"I have some students coming now, Alex. Perhaps you've ridden enough for your first time anyhow," she called. "Take them back in."

Sam got Echo turned and through the stable door and finally stopped. Then she did her best to reverse the process she had gone through when she mounted. But, just as she was feeling triumphant, her foot caught in the reins. As she lost her balance, she caught at Echo but there was no handhold. Her whole body went stiff. With a swoosh and a bump, she sprawled in an ignominious heap at Aunt Mary's feet.

"Oww!" Sam yelped as every bone in her body felt the impact.

Echo nosed her comfortingly but it did not take away the shame she felt. Her face flamed as, ignoring her painful elbows and knees, she scrambled to her feet.

With every atom of her being, she fought not to burst into tears. Out of the corner of her eye, she caught sight of Bethany trying to hide a grin. Then Thomas came dancing out and saved her.

"Alice, somebody called you on the phone. She left a message," he said in his small cheery voice.

Sam's heart leapt. It had to be Alex. She didn't know anyone else who would call her here.

"Alex, are you all right?" Aunt Mary asked. She did not sound terribly worried. Sam bit her lip and then said as jauntily as she could that she was fine.

"I'll look after Echo for you then. You run along," the woman said, taking Echo's rein and leading him away.

It had not crossed Sam's mind that she should unsaddle Echo and put her back in her stall. She would have to find out exactly what was expected of her before next time.

Thankfully, she took off at a hobbling run.

She dialled the number Thomas had printed so carefully. It rang four times, then five, then six. She was going to hang up when an old man's shaky voice answered.

"George Carr here."

Sam was taken aback. Who on earth was George Carr?

"Is … Sam there?" she asked after a long moment.

"No, she is not. She had to go back to the Truebloods'. I live next door. She'll be back in the morning. Call then, Sam. You'll be able to speak freely. Goodbye."

The old cracked voice chuckled and the line was disconnected. Sam stared at the receiver in her own hand. She was not sure why but she felt bewildered and outraged. What was wrong? Then her heart skipped a beat.

He had called her Sam.

"What's the matter, Alice?" Thomas asked.

Sam stared down at his small bright face.

"Nothing's wrong," she said. But neither of them believed it.

"I'll find out," he murmured, his eyes sparkling. "I always do."

That night, Sam no longer felt homesick but every muscle in her body seemed to be aching. And her thoughts pounded around and around like hamsters on a treadmill. What had Alex done? Had she blabbed the whole scheme? Sam had not known how much she wanted to ride Echo again until she thought she might never have another chance.

What would Aunt Mary do if she were told the truth? Would she hit the roof?

Sam made a face in the dark.

How could you, Alex? she asked inside her head. How could you tell my secret as well as your own? I should have guessed you'd ruin everything.

The next morning, as soon as breakfast was over and the others were preoccupied, Sam tried the number again.

This time, Alex herself answered.

"Hi, Alex, old thing. How's Horse Heaven?" she asked at once.

"You told! How could you?" Sam burst out, keeping her voice down with difficulty. "I should have known you couldn't be trusted."

Alex gasped. Then words spilled out in a rush.

"It's okay. You won't mind when I explain. Mr. Carr can keep a secret. He says he's kept lots. And when we're at his place, we won't have to pretend, Sam. We can be our real selves."

Sam sucked in a deep breath and got ready to go on raging. Then she took in what Alex had said and deflated like a pricked balloon.

"Well, maybe it'll be okay then," she said, keeping her voice low in spite of a longing to shout.

Thomas, who had stuck to her like a burr ever since she came to the phone, had now moved away but not very far. Hearing Sam laugh a moment later, he crept closer and watched with interest as Sam began to murmur to the person on the other end of the line.

"Are you used to it yet?" she asked.

The small boy sat down on the stairs to listen harder. It was mysterious. People frequently tried to keep secrets from him but he almost always discovered what they were trying to hide. When he had answered the phone the day before, the girl had said, "Could I speak to Sam—uh, Alex, please?"

Why?

And then there were the shoes.... The name inked inside them started with an *S*.

"Quit eavesdropping, Thomas Grantham," Sam said suddenly.

He gave her an injured look out of wide brown eyes.

"I am not," he lied, and stalked away, pretending to be deeply hurt.

Sam was not fooled. She watched him go and laughed aloud.

"If I ever tell, it'll be to Thomas," she said. "He'd make a great detective."

11

lex got up too early to go over to Mr. Carr's. She played with the papillons and watched the clock. On the dot of nine, she ran across the yard to peer over the fence.

The old man was watching for her.

"Come on through," he called in a gruff voice that did not match the smile in his deep-set eyes.

They went inside at once to wait for Sam's call. Mr. Carr, leading the way, still looked far from spry but he did seem more lively. While they waited for the phone to ring, Alex took in details she had totally missed the day before. The books, for instance. One set of bookcases was full of fantasies. The trilogy by Garth Nix that she had just finished was there. It was one of the best sets of books she had ever read. There were some books about birds. And there was a whole bookcase filled with murder mysteries. Suddenly Alex let out a yelp.

"You have *Fatal Error* by David Scott!" she cried, pulling the book down and opening it eagerly.

There it was, the dedication: "To Sam, who done it."

Mr. Carr glanced at her and raised his bushy eyebrows in question marks.

"It's by Sam's father," Alex explained, delighted that she need not invent a bit to account for her interest. "Look."

She held out the book opened to the dedication.

"I think I remember it," Mr. Carr said. "It's clever. And it got some good reviews. It has a pug dog in it. My wife thought the dog was the best thing about the story. The dog's name is Samson but they call him Sam for short!"

Alex laughed so hard she collapsed onto the nearest chair.

"Does Sam solve the mystery?" she asked.

"I don't think so, but he finds the body," Mr. Carr said. "I think it's hidden in the privy."

Then the phone rang.

It was wonderful to be able to speak freely to Sam even if she did begin by being furious. The old man seemed to be getting a tremendous kick out of sharing their secret. He sat in his deep armchair by the fireplace and grinned at her as they talked.

She soon understood that Sam had an eavesdropper at her end.

"Is someone listening?" she asked to make sure.

"Just Thomas. He's nearly six and we're friends."

"Does he know about …"

"Not yet, although his ears are sticking out so far they're flapping," Sam said. "Never mind Thomas. How are things with you?"

As they told each other what had happened since they left the airport, Alex looked down at the table beside Mr. Carr's chair. She saw at once that it was on wheels and could be swung across his lap with ease. On it was a piece of paper with several long words written out, words that were definitely not English.

Alex tipped her head to see them better. Dad had told her she had an excellent vocabulary. Yet she could make no sense out of these words. She stopped listening to Sam for a moment and stared at them.

Lasata lalaithamin Loving to hear you laugh
Maw gov annen Well met
Namaarie Farewell
Tennateywan Until later

"Sam, are you listening?" Sam's voice demanded.

"Yes, of course I'm listening," Alex said, looking away so she could concentrate.

When she looked back, Mr. Carr had written at the bottom of the page, "They're Elvish."

"Oh," Alex said, amazed. Then she told Sam, "I'll explain to you when I see you. When can you come over?"

The two of them arranged to meet that afternoon. Sam said she could borrow Kenneth's old bike, which he was not using.

"Did you tell him why?" Alex asked.

"Sort of. I said we'd made friends on the plane and we wanted to get together sometime. Even Aunt Mary thought it was fine. They really like your Mrs. Trueblood."

"She's great," Alex agreed.

After they hung up, Alex went on staring at the mysterious words.

"How come you know words in Elvish?" she demanded.

Mr. Carr peered up at her from under his shaggy brows. But finally he said gruffly, "I like to keep my hand in. My wife ... she claimed to be descended from an elf. I wanted to put the one about loving to hear your laughter on her tombstone but the minister thought it was weird and so I didn't. I was afraid my nephew might use it to prove I was insane and should be locked up."

"How do you know the words?" Alex began, wondering if he really was what Dad called "touched."

"Tolkien, of course," he said so matter-of-factly that she knew he was as sane as her father or Margaret Trueblood.

Then he showed her the list of mysterious words again and Alex instantly grew exultant.

"That's exactly what Sam and I need," she said. "Our own secret language."

"You and the elves," Mr. Carr chuckled. "If you come across Legalas, you'll be all ready to chat. They're actually pretty long and complicated. My wife and I memorized a few and stuck to them. We never tried whole conversations."

"Sam's coming over on Kenneth's bike," Alex told him. "I wish there was a bike I could borrow but Sam is sure Josie's would be too small."

"I was about to suggest a solution. My wife used to ride a bike when she went into town. You're welcome to borrow it. I think it will be the right size for you."

"I'm small for my age," Alex said doubtfully.

"So was she," he said. "After all, she said she was descended from elves. It's a child's machine. You try it and see. I called Mrs. Trueblood and asked her if it would be all right for you to have it. She said it was fine with her as long as you checked in before going on any very distant journeys. She's a most satisfactory neighbour."

"She sure is," Alex said, gazing at him with startled eyes. When had he called? Then she remembered the time she had spent curled up on her bed with a book called *Jane of Lantern Hill*, which she had found in her room. She had believed she had read all of L.M. Montgomery's novels and could not think how she had missed this one. She would not have heard the phone ringing during the hours she had spent on Prince Edward Island with Jane. Jane's father was so like Dad.

George Carr chuckled at her astonished look.

"It'll be in the shed out back. I hope the tires are all right. If not, there's a pump there."

When Sam came after lunch, Alex told her about Mrs. Carr's bicycle. They dug it out and stared at it. It was pink! It was decidedly not intended for an adult.

"It'll be just right for you," Sam said, "and the tires are only a bit soft."

They wheeled it out to the driveway. Margaret Trueblood came out to be properly introduced to Sam, whom Alex remembered to call Alex just in time. Margaret studied her for a long moment, so long that Sam wondered if her face were extra dirty or something. Then she smiled and said, "So let's see a demonstration of your cycling skill."

Alex had a bike but rarely rode it, so she was slightly nervous. Mr. Carr was watching, too, from his front window. She wobbled badly for a moment or two but then it came back to her and she flew down the paved drive and back like a bird.

"Perfect," Margaret Trueblood said. "Now I must go back to work. Nice to have met you, Alex."

Her face still wore a strange expression but she waved to Mr. Carr and went back to bathing dogs.

Alex wanted to keep going down the road with Sam beside her but they went back into George Carr's house instead. He laughed at the stumbling introduction he had heard Alex make. "If the two of you get through the summer without giving yourselves away, you'll flabbergast me," he said. "You've taken on a great game of 'Let's pretend.'"

"Can you tell her about the Elvish words?" Alex said, changing the subject fast. "I want Sam to see."

Before the week was out, Sam and Alex had learned the words Mrs. and Mr. Carr had liked best, plus two or three more. After that, Alex invented another half-dozen.

"We should make up elf names," she said, her eyes shining.

"Forget it," Sam told her with a grin. "I'm having enough trouble being Alexis, Alex, and Alice. I'm not going to answer to Samolass or Galadrisam."

"I didn't know you'd read *The Lord of the Rings*," Alex said, impressed.

"Are you kidding? Dad read all three books aloud to me," Sam said. "I loved hearing them but no way would I actually read that many pages of anything. Whenever I tell him I'm bored, he offers to start reading me *War and Peace*. But he backs down every time because, according to him, you have to be at least fourteen to get it."

The most important word Alex came up with was *regnad*, which was their favourite word of warning.

When Thomas heard it, he made Sam write it down for him and, half an hour later, he raced up to her, eyes sparkling.

"It's just 'danger' backwards," he crowed. "I told you you can't keep secrets from me."

Sam and Alex explored the whole neighbourhood on their borrowed bikes. Mr. Carr's house became their meeting place. Margaret Trueblood was delighted that they were spending so much time with the lonely old man. She never once asked what they were up to when they were there. Mostly they talked. Sometimes they played Scrabble. He also taught them to play cribbage and backgammon.

Every so often, the girls heard the distant puzzling voices saying mysterious things but Mr. Carr kept the door to the basement shut tight and never allowed them to go down there.

One morning, however, he did tell them they could go back into his garden shed.

"I believe you will find a treasure waiting propped against the rear wall," he said, acting mysterious.

They found the treasure finally: a tent!

It was covered with dust and extremely hard to extricate from the ladder and lawnmower and snow shovel and rakes and hoes that were stacked all around it. They raced back to the cottage, highly excited and covered with filth.

"You have my permission to pitch it in the yard if you think you can manage it," he said, delighted by their wild joy.

They went right to work on it. After several false starts and pinched fingers, they got it up. It was great. It had a double door, one screen to keep out bugs, and a window flap in its back wall. It was big enough for them to use as a clubhouse.

"I feel as though we've had an extra birthday each," Sam told Mr. Carr.

"Good," he growled, his eyes twinkling. "See you don't crash the bike or …"

He was stuck for a tent disaster.

"We'll be extremely careful," Alex promised.

Sam brought Thomas over to see the tent one day and, afterwards, had to let Kenneth and Josie visit too, but they did not keep coming. It was too far for the little ones to come on their own and Kenneth had now started attending soccer camp most of the day.

One morning Alex biked over to the Granthams' to tell Sam she had had a long-distance phone call the night before.

Sam had just come in from riding Echo and her thoughts were far away from her old life until Alex's words penetrated. Then she felt sudden terror clutch her heart.

"Don't worry. It was your grandma's next-door neighbour to say that your grandmother is home and doing fine. She didn't write to you because she got pneumonia while she was in the hospital but she's all right now. She still has pain and she's getting therapy and going to stay at a rehab place. But she'll get in touch as soon as she feels better."

"What on earth did you tell her about me?" Sam demanded, her eyes round with alarm.

"I just pretended I *was* you, the way I do every day," Alex said. "Your grandma would have known better but this other woman never suspected a thing. 'Give her my love,' I said and she said she would."

"Wow! I never thought of someone phoning," Sam said with a gulp.

"You can write and tell her you'll phone her in a week or so. Mr. Carr would let you. Then you could hear her voice and both of you would feel better."

"It hasn't been difficult so far," Sam said. "My dad's too busy to write, and it's been simple to deliver your mother's one postcard," Sam laughed. She felt relieved about her grandmother—and relieved that both she and Alex had the kind of parents they did.

"I keep expecting something dire to happen but so far, so good," Alex answered. "Hey! How would you like to sleep out in the tent?"

Sam jumped in the air and clapped her hands above her head.

"Right on!" she yelled.

wrong way. They had been in the tent while the girls were setting it up, and clearly they had decided it was a safe house for papillons.

Sam knew that she would never be terrified by lightning again. In awe, yes. Careful, certainly. But not hysterical. She would just have to remember Alex saying, "We need Jesus."

"What for?" Sam had demanded, snuggling Peony to her.

"He could say, 'Peace! Be still!'"

Sam had then pointed one finger at the tent flap and intoned, "Peace! Be still!"

And the storm had started to move off. Oh, there were a few faint rumbles and faraway flashes, but no more bad ones.

"I never would have guessed you had such power," Alex had teased.

"Believe it," Sam said loftily and giggled.

"Do you realize we've kept our secret for weeks? It's August already!" Alex said after a while. "I was positive we'd give it all away long before this."

"Mrs. Trueblood has a way of looking at me that makes me wonder sometimes," Sam said slowly.

"Mr. Carr's knowing sure helps," Alex said. "I don't think Margaret has guessed. Maybe she's noticing your hair."

"What about my hair?"

"Well, it was short when we got here," yawned Alex. "Margaret said you need to get it trimmed soon."

Sam tried to be annoyed but she was sliding into sleep. "Goo' night," she mumbled.

The papillons wagged their tails in the darkness but Alex made no response at all.

Five seconds later, they were both deep in slumber.

Mr. Carr hobbled out with a walker to wish them good morning and found them still fast asleep after having spent so much of the night wide awake. He was having none of that.

"Get up, you slugabeds, and help me pick some raspberries for my breakfast," he commanded.

They came staggering out and accompanied him to his thicket of prickly raspberry canes. Alex completely understood his wish not to get too near after his close encounter with the rose bush.

After they had spent that night on proper mattresses, they decided to sleep in the tent again.

"It's so nice not to be worried all the time about spilling the beans," Alex said. "We can say anything in the tent."

Later, Margaret Trueblood said to Alex, "You mean so much to the old fellow this summer, Sam. He positively grinned at me just now when I met him eating raspberries. He had a big bowlful. Did you help pick them?"

"Could be," Alex said. "Alex helped a bit."

Sam had begged her to come over to the Granthams' and see how she had improved in her riding. Alex put it off as long as she could. She was pleased Sam was happy but she did not want to meet the horses up close. Finally she had to agree to go, though.

She pedalled the pink bike over to the Granthams' as slowly as possible. Watching her friend's joy and pride as she trotted by, she was glad they had made the big swap. She was thankful not only for Sam's sake but for her own. She still found horses alarming.

"This is Beauregard," Sam told her proudly. "Uncle Duncan rides him and, when he's away, Aunt Mary does. Isn't he something!"

"Yeah," Alex said with a shiver Sam missed.

In Alex's opinion, the stallion was not a mere horse, he was a nightmare. That very night, safe in her own bed, away from Heron Hill, she dreamed he had come thundering after her in some dream meadow and her feet were stuck to the ground. The papillons, worried by her moaning, licked her nose and woke her.

"Thank you, thank you," she gasped, cuddling their small bodies. "How did I ever get along before we met?"

And, suddenly, she knew that the summer was going to end and she was going to have to leave them, and she blinked back tears. How was she going to bear life in the beige townhouse after this?

13

*T*hen, two weeks into August, Alex went next door one morning to find no sign of Mr. Carr. He had given her a key so he need not get up from his chair to let her in. But he had always called out a greeting before. She knocked once and then knocked again and waited.

Silence.

At last, she fitted the key into the lock and eased the door open.

"Mr. Carr, it's me," she called and waited, her heart thumping.

Still there was no answering call.

Slowly, unwillingly, she went through the kitchen into the front room. He was not in his chair. His walker was not in its usual place.

Then she turned and saw the basement door, the one he had never once opened in her presence, standing ajar.

She stood stock-still for a few heartbeats and then ran, her knees shaking, to investigate. He was there, lying in a heap at the bottom of the stairs. She started to cry when she saw that his face was grey. He looked … dead.

Was he breathing? She could not tell. Her hands were far too unsteady to check for a pulse, and her eyes were dimmed by terror and tears. But she must get help.

She raced to the telephone and dialled first 911 and then the Truebloods.

"Stay with him. I'll be right over," Margaret said, and hung up.

She was as good as her word. She knelt beside him and felt his bony wrist.

"He's alive," she said, "but his pulse is very weak. Get a blanket, Sam."

It seemed to take years for the ambulance to arrive. The siren was going full blast. Alex was impressed. It sounded like the sirens on TV. The paramedics carried him out on a stretcher. Alex, still crying, stood at the door ready to wave.

"I'll come and see you later," she said loudly, leaning close as he was carried past.

He opened his eyes and spoke. It was only one or two slurred words.

Alex did not understand him. He repeated it once more as they loaded the stretcher into the ambulance.

"What was that?" Margaret asked.

"I don't know," Alex agonized.

"It didn't make sense," said the ambulance man. "It was something like 'Tuppence a bag.' He's hallucinating, I'm afraid. They often do."

Alex saw Mr. Carr's eyes grow angry. He had not been rambling.

"I heard you," she called after him.

But she still did not understand.

"I think he'll be in Intensive Care. I doubt they'll let us in, since we're not relatives. I don't think they'll let children in either," Margaret said, giving Alex a big hug. When Alex pulled away, after drenching Margaret's shirtfront with tears, she went right to the phone to call Sam.

"He'll be in Intensive Care and only relatives will be allowed to visit," she sobbed.

"Nuts to that. We can say we're great-nieces," Sam said.

"I thought of that but Margaret thinks, even if we did, they won't let children in," Alex said. "Can you come over?"

"I'll be there in fifteen minutes," Sam declared. She arrived in ten. They went up to Alex's room, Pee and Milkweed on their heels. Alex plunked herself down on the bed and mopped her eyes with the corner of the sheet.

"He's like our grandfather," she said.

"I know," Sam said, although she did not feel quite as close to the old man as Alex did.

"He was already sick," Alex mumbled. "He told me he had Parkinson's. Can that kill you?"

"I don't know," Sam said miserably. "I don't think so … but I don't know."

Just sitting around feeling stricken got on Sam's nerves at last.

"Let's go over to my place and go to the river. It's neat there and we can wade. It's so hot today."

Part of Alex wanted to stay where she was, grieving and keeping vigil, but another part longed to escape.

"Go along, child," Margaret said. "There's nothing you can do here."

It was a relief to leave the neighbourhood of the tragedy. At the farm, Thomas and Josie joined them and they all went wading. When Kenneth came home from his day camp, they began working on a dam.

"Maybe we could dam it up and make a swimming place," Sam suggested.

Their dam was impressive but, just as they were making a sizeable pool, Kenneth decided they must not block the creek completely or the neighbours would be unhappy.

"There would be a flood in the end," Josie surprised them by announcing.

Thomas tied their sneakers together with their laces and ran off laughing when they tried to make him undo his mischief.

Alex arrived back at the Truebloods' dirty and tired and even happy as long as she kept her eyes turned away from the deserted cottage next door.

The next morning, though, word came from the hospital that Mr. Carr was still in Intensive Care and very ill. He had had a stroke. His nephew had been notified. He could not come at once but he would be there as soon as he could manage it.

"Oh, no!" Alex cried. "Mr. Carr doesn't like him. He wants to put him in an old people's place."

"He'll have to go somewhere, if he recovers. He won't be able to keep on living alone after this," Margaret said. Then, after a moment's hesitation, she looked at Alex and added quietly, "I think you should know that his chances of recovery are slim. The doctor told Daniel he's been drifting in and out of consciousness most of the time since yesterday. And he's growing weaker, not stronger, with every hour that passes. The nephew is his only close relative. Personally I think the old fellow would be glad to go."

Alex felt sick. She called Sam and asked her to forget her horses and come over. Sam was annoyed. She was sincerely sorry about Mr. Carr but she was getting to be a good rider and Bethany had said Sam might come and ride Echo down the road while she was out exercising Melody. Sam was opening her mouth to tell Alex she would have to wait when Bethany ran up and said her mother was taking her shopping so they would exercise the horses later.

"Okay," Sam said into the phone. She was still in a bad mood when she reached the Truebloods' but one look at Alex's tear-streaked face changed all that.

"He'll be okay," she said, putting an arm around her friend.

"No," Alex whispered. "Margaret says he may not want to go on living."

The two of them went outside, away from Margaret's concerned gaze. She might find a chore for them to do if they were just sitting around. They ended up staring over the gate at the cottage next door.

"Let's go over," Alex said. "Maybe we could water the lawn or something."

That was how they were together when they heard bizarre voices coming through the basement window of the empty house.

"Hurry up. Hurry up. George, hurry."

Alex and Sam froze, turning their heads only to look into each other's wide eyes.

"I heard that voice before," Alex whispered. "He said it must be the radio."

"But why would he have a radio playing in the basement?" Sam asked.

Then they heard a phone ring.

"Hello," said another voice. "Hello, hello."

The phone rang again twice.

Then a totally different voice gave a deep, rumbling laugh. All the voices were coming through the same window, which was open a couple of inches. Alex was sure it had not been open before.

"Who ..." she squeaked.

"I see you, George," the first voice said. "I see you. Blah, blah, blah. Don't give me that. Hurry up, I say."

Sam's fingers gripped Alex's wrist like talons.

"Somebody's in there," she whispered.

"More than one," Alex whispered back.

There was a babble of meaningless sounds now. Then a banging of something striking metal. Then came a truly blood-curdling scream.

The scream was what did it. Sam and Alex did not stop running until they were safely inside the Truebloods' back hall.

"Should we call the police?" Alex asked.

But, all at once, Sam had turned to stare back at the old house with a strange expression on her face.

"Did you catch the last few words while we were running?" she asked slowly, the terror in her eyes making way for something entirely different, a look of speculation.

Alex shook her head. She couldn't trust her voice.

"I think it said, 'No crackers for me,'" Sam said. "Alex, come on. Let's go back and investigate."

"Are you crazy? No crackers for me," Alex repeated, blankly. "So what? That's crazy!"

"It could be a budgie," Sam said. "Maybe, instead of teaching it to say, 'Polly wants a cracker!' they taught it, 'No crackers for me.'"

"It screamed," Alex reminded her. "It sounded as though … as though …"

Sam glanced at her friend's pale face. She knew how that scream had sounded. Like the horror shows on TV, like somebody facing a vampire or a serial killer. Blood-curdling. But did vampires say, "No crackers for me"? Or "Hurry up, George"?

"I saw a show about parrots on PBS," she said. "They scream all the time. It can't hurt to at least go back. But if it isn't a parrot, it's people. And there's something wrong with them."

Alex had vampires in mind too but she couldn't imagine one of them saying, "Hurry up, George." Unless …

"Come on, Alex," Sam urged. "Before I lose my nerve."

"I'm coming," said Alex weakly, and she trailed after her brave friend. As she did, she was remembering an old voice croaking, "Tuppence a bag."

14

When they reached the back door, Alex hesitated. Then she pulled up the key, which hung on a string around her neck. The last time she had let herself in, she had found the old man unconscious. Remembering, she froze.

"Come on!" Sam urged, trying to hide her growing panic with a bossy tone.

Alex fixed her with a glare.

Far away, they could hear a chime ring out. Then someone began to sing.

Alex was ready to run again but Sam gave her a look of such scorn that she stood her ground. They listened for footsteps. The house was silent.

Silent as a tomb, Sam thought but did not say.

Then Alex spotted the outside cellar door. It sloped up

from the ground like the one in the old song her mother had learned when she was a child.

Holler down my rain barrel.
Slide down my cellar door …

You could have slid down Mr. Carr's door if you didn't mind getting splinters in your rear end. The wood was rough and covered with peeling paint.

"Let's try this way," Alex said, dropping the key back out of sight.

She ran over and tugged at the iron handle. The door creaked open two inches and then stuck fast. From the crack leading down into darkness, a voice called, "Hello, hello. Come on in. No crackers for me. Ha, ha, ha!"

Alex dropped the heavy door with a thud.

"That's no budgie," she said hoarsely.

"No. I think it is a bird, though," Sam said, sounding much more cheerful. "Come on. We've got to get the door open."

It took them fifteen minutes. Nobody had opened that door for a long time. They yanked and tugged. Alex ran back to the Truebloods' for a big knife and a hammer. They had to bang and chop at stuck places. But, at last, the door creaked up halfway.

"That'll do it," Sam said. "We can get in. You go first, Marco Polo."

Alex was about to say, "No way, José!" Then she realized she was going to have to do this thing. She didn't want Sam getting all the credit and teasing her forever after.

She slid through the opening and onto a step. Sam was right behind her. The door at the bottom of the steps stood ajar. Beyond was darkness.

"Okay," Sam whispered, then added, "Why didn't we bring a flashlight?"

Alex could not speak. She ran her hand over the wall and found a light switch. She pushed it up. A dusty light bulb dangling from the ceiling came on. The light it shed was feeble but it showed them a basement room like a million others. It was dingy and a bit damp and full of junk. Nothing there looked as though it contained treasure.

They stood staring around, not wanting to leave the safety of the dim room. They were already in trouble if they were caught.

"I see you, George. Hurry up. Come on. Merry Christmas," said the first voice they had heard.

It was a woman's voice, Alex realized, but not quite real.

"Let's get it over with," Sam said. "There are probably more switches in there."

Side by side, they marched through a wide doorway into another room and there, staring at them from inside a large square cage, was a grey parrot with a red tail and beady eyes that pinned them to the wall.

"Hello, hello," he said. "I'm Bilbo Baggins.... George.... Do shut up, Bilbo, or I'll wring your neck.... George, don't tease the bird."

In between the words there were squeaks and squawks and two hiccups and one loud burp.

"It's an African Grey!" Sam breathed. "They're the best talkers. I saw them on that TV show."

All Alex's terror blew away like dandelion fluff. She gave a huge sigh followed by a shaky laugh.

"Don't say 'it.' *He* is an African Grey. Hello, Bilbo Baggins. I thought you were a hobbit," Alex said. "Oh, Sam, the poor boy. He needs fresh water. And food. He must be starving."

The parrot's cage was stocked with metal food and water dishes. He had eaten almost all the food, and two of the water dishes were half-full of scummy water. But beneath the table the cage sat on were big glass jars filled with seeds, nuts, and pellets.

"Maybe Mr. Carr was on his way to feed him yesterday when he collapsed," Sam said. Then, wrinkling her nose she said, "Yuck! Bilbo pooped in his water dish."

"He didn't know Mr. Carr wouldn't be coming home. Sam, Mr. Carr can't talk. If he can think, he must be worried sick about his parrot."

And then the light began to dawn on Alex. "'Tuppence a bag'!" she said. "Sam, get it? Mr. Carr said, 'Tuppence a bag' when they were carrying him to the ambulance. It's in *Mary Poppins*. It goes, 'Feed the birds, tuppence a bag.'" Sam began to sing.

"He was telling us. If he'd just said, 'Feed the bird' …"

"We'd never have figured it out anyway," Alex said. "We didn't know there was a bird."

Sam slid out one of the food dishes, took some peanuts in their shells from one of the jars, and put them in the dish. Suddenly, as she put the dish back in place, Bilbo's beak came down like lightning, just missing her finger.

"Yikes!" she yelped, jumping back.

"It wasn't you he was after, it was the peanut," Alex said, watching the parrot holding the peanut in his left foot. He broke the shell with his beak and then began to take out the nut a bit at a time. When the end of the peanut was freed from the shell, he delicately removed it with his beak and ate it. Then he got out a second peanut just as tidily.

"Wow," Sam said. "He uses his claw like a hand."

"Bilbo Baggins is a clever bird," Alex crooned. "Such a smart bird."

Bilbo tipped his head sideways and stared at her. He did not say a word. But he was definitely listening. Every feather seemed to quiver with attention.

He kept silent until Alex turned away to get him some of the pellets in the other big jar.

"Such a clever bird!" he said smugly. "Isn't he clever, George?"

"George must be Mr. Carr," Alex said.

"I'll bet you're right. Alex, are you thinking what I'm thinking?"

"I'm afraid so," Alex said. "We have to go visit Mr. Carr, no matter what anyone says. Is that what you're thinking?"

"Right," Sam said. "If he can't talk to us, he still might hear that we found Bilbo and be glad. What do you think he'll say?"

"I can't imagine," Alex said, staring at the parrot as though he were a unicorn or a mermaid.

"Well, we have to go," Sam said firmly. "We have to go fast. What if the old guy dies? He must be so worried."

Alex knew Sam was right but she was still angry at George Carr as well as sorry for him. He had kept his parrot in the basement and not told them about him in all these weeks since they had come to Guelph. Why? He must have known they would love Bilbo.

"Okay, okay," she growled. "How will we get there? I don't want to tell the Truebloods."

Sam looked thoughtful.

"Me neither," she said at last. "I mean, I don't want my bunch to know either. They'd take it all out of our hands. But we could bike there."

Alex's face lit up.

"You are a genius," she breathed.

"I wondered when you'd notice," Sam said, her face deadpan. "I'll call and say you've invited me to lunch. You can call the Truebloods and tell them the same thing. But see if you can get something for us to eat before we go. Aunt Mary made me take a cell phone with me in case I got into trouble. You can use it."

"Do you know where the hospital is?" Alex asked, feeling a little dizzy at the speed with which Sam was settling everything.

"Yes," Sam said. "We drove Bethany up there to do her candy-striping."

Sam ran into the old man's bedroom and came back with a pair of clean pyjamas in a bag.

"We'll say we were asked to bring them for him."

Alex was astonished by the thoroughness of Sam's planning.

"Perfect," she said. "Let's go before we get caught."

Everything worked like clockwork. Margaret Trueblood sounded pleased, as though that was one less thing she had to worry about. Sam's hostess was a bit more suspicious but Sam talked her around, asking if she would like to speak to Sam personally.

They got lost twice on their way to the hospital. Sam, who, despite her wild hair, looked a bit more presentable than Alex, went to the Information Desk and asked where

Mr. Carr's room was. She waved the bag with the pair of pyjamas in it. The nurse at the desk nodded.

"That's nice, dear, but don't stay too long. He's a sick man even if he has been moved to the Acute Care floor. His nephew asked that he be given a private room," she said. She had blue hair in neat waves, and glasses on a cord around her neck, and she waved her hands in the air while she talked. Sam did not trust her but trust was not important. The woman only noticed them with a tiny bit of her busy mind. She answered the phone twice while they were standing by her desk. She wrote the room number on a slip of paper and pushed it across to them. "He'll be glad to see his granddaughter, I'm sure."

Sam's face was red as she turned away and beckoned Alex to follow her. They located Mr. Carr without exchanging any more words. They crept into the shadowed room. The shrunken body on the bed looked dead except that his breath was giving a thin whistle each time it came out of his open mouth. His face was a mass of wrinkles interrupted by a long nose and two craggy white eyebrows. His top teeth were missing.

Now what? Alex thought. Why had they come? It was not going to work. Mr. Carr looked dead already.

Then she remembered Bilbo Baggins with his food running out and his dirty water.

"Mr. Carr," she burst out, "we've found your Bilbo. He's still alive. We haven't told anybody about him yet. But ..."

She stopped dead as the old man's eyes snapped open. He stared at her. The stare looked a bit like the parrot's, piercing and unnerving.

"Silly bird," he said, slurring the words so much they were hard to understand. "My wife's. Made ... me mad. Talked like her: 'Hurry up, George.' Made me lonesome. Feed him, did you? Put him downstairs for peace. Tried to tell. Said. Tuppence a bag. Did you get ..."

"We got it," Alex said hastily. She had been mad at him for not telling them about his parrot but Bilbo did keep talking in what was clearly Mrs. Carr's voice. It *would* make you lonesome. Anyway, she could not stay mad at this clearly very sick, shrunken old man, so alone in the world. The blurred, whispering words trailed away. Mr. Carr was asleep once more. He had left them high and dry. His worried visitors stared at each other in consternation. Now what?

Then he spoke once more, without opening his eyes.

"Yours," Mr. Carr said. "I gave envelope to Mrs. ... Mrs. ..."

"Trueblood?" Alex said, trying to help.

"Blood.... House to nephew, bird to you. Had a feeling something might happen.... Tired."

Alex, with tears welling up in her eyes, moved close to him and leaned down so he would be certain to know her. He half-opened his eyes and gazed back at her as he had done long ago when he had been trapped in the rose bush. And she saw, in that instant, he was afraid. Her hand closed over his and they clung together.

Then a nurse rustled in with a thermometer in her hand.

"Run along, children," she said. "Mr. Carr isn't up to visitors just now. I don't know who let you in."

"But—" Alex began to argue.

"Waste of time," said the old voice from the bed. "She … won't listen. Go."

"Now, now," the nurse began, in a hard voice smothered in syrup.

"Get away." The old man did his best to yell at her. It sounded feeble but it meant business. "Leave me be, you Jezebel."

Outside the door, Sam and Alex grinned at each other and took off as fast as they could go. They had plans to make, things to think through. And they did not want to be caught and questioned until they were ready.

"I wonder how long we have before they catch us," Sam said, standing by the bike rack outside the hospital.

"Mrs. Trueblood told me his nephew is coming. She didn't know when. He might come right away if they decide Mr. Carr is … is …"

"He seemed pretty lively to me," Sam said. But he had not really been lively. His voice had sounded like a paper voice, not a real one. And his skin had had no colour.

Alex looked at her and then looked away.

"I still don't know what we should do," she said. "But I'm going back to see Bilbo right now. I think he's cool! And lonely. Mr. Carr told us to take care of him. So we will."

"I can't come now," Sam told her. "I'm having a riding lesson in two minutes, and if I don't show up they'll wonder what happened to me."

Alex tried to look sorry. She *was* sorry in a way. The Carrs' house was eerie even with Bilbo livening it up. Having Sam along for company would have been comforting. But she also wanted to be alone with the parrot. She wanted to see if they could make friends. Making friends with a wild creature like a parrot was a different thing from petting Mrs. Trueblood's butterfly dogs or stroking old Merc. It was unnerving. It would be an adventure—if she did not get bitten. She longed to find out if she could do it, if Bilbo would be responsive.

"Have fun," she said. "I'll call you tomorrow and we can figure out what comes next."

They picked up their bikes and rode off together, going their separate ways as they reached Sam's. Sam was heading for Echo and Alex was almost certain Bilbo Baggins was watching out for her return. They had no time to waste on idle chat. They had swapped lives and they had gotten through a whole month and a half of masquerading without being caught. It was working. Life had never seemed so full of promise.

Or so deliciously dangerous.

Or so sad, Alex thought, remembering the old eyes that had looked so afraid.

15

Sam felt flustered. She was a minute or so late for her lesson when she pulled up. It felt like hours since she had left. Bethany must be mad as a hornet. But once she had put the bike away, she found the house empty.

The family must be out with the horses. She ran to join them and discovered Bethany mounted on Echo, trotting smoothly around the track.

Sam would have been envious a few weeks before but she rode with much greater confidence now. She was not as impressed as she had been at first. But she was annoyed that Bethany had grabbed the chance to saddle up Echo.

She was about to lead out another horse when Aunt Mary told her that Bethany was going to have to dismount and help with a family group who were coming to see over the place so they could decide about sending their girls to the last session of summer riding camp.

Sam did her best to hide her disappointment. But after all, nobody was paying for her lessons. She went back to the house and was up in her room reading when, an hour later, Josie called her.

"Your friend Sam is outside. She told me to tell you Bilbo needs help."

Sam dropped her book and clattered down the stairs.

"Who is this boy?" Aunt Mary said, catching her arm as she made for the door.

"Not a boy—Samantha, remember? From the Truebloods'?"

"Oh, that child," Aunt Mary said. "But who is Bill?"

"He lives next door to the Truebloods," Sam told her. "We only just met him."

Sam turned away so she would not have to answer more questions. She and Alex had decided long ago that the safest thing was to keep the families apart as much as possible and to answer any questions with the shortest answers they could think up. Otherwise, they were sure to blow it. By this time, she felt pretty sure she could keep the secret but sometimes it had been a close thing.

"Sam is waiting!" Josie interrupted. They were not listening to her and she sounded fed up with all of them.

"No kid lives next door to the Truebloods, just an old couple," Bethany muttered as Sam started for the door again.

"Bilbo isn't a boy exactly," Sam said over her shoulder. "May I go talk to her, Aunt Mary?"

"Of course," Aunt Mary said, but she sounded flustered.

Sam ran down the hall and burst out the front door. She looked around for Alex, certain she must be gone. But she was standing by the hedge.

"What's wrong with Bilbo?" Sam hissed, afraid one of the Granthams was listening.

"We have to find a place to move him to. I heard Margaret on the phone telling Daniel that the nephew is on his way. She also said Mr. Carr lapsed into a coma and he's not expected to last the night."

"But ... but ... he talked to us," Sam gasped.

"It must have happened right after we left. Anyway, what will we do?"

"I don't think Aunt Mary would let me take in a parrot here, and Bethany would have a fit. Besides, I don't want to explain. Did you ask Mrs. Trueblood about that envelope?"

"I forgot. But I can't stay," Alex said. "Meet me at the Carrs' place as soon as you can get away. And *think*, Sam, or he'll sell our parrot for sure. I saw an ad in the paper today for an African Grey. They're worth one thousand dollars! He'd sell Bilbo like a shot—and Mr. Carr said we were to keep him. You heard him."

She got on her bike and pedalled away, leaving Sam staring after her. What she had said was true. Alex had heard the old man telling them, loud and clear, that they were to take his bird and keep him. But they couldn't. No way.

One thousand dollars!

Go back to the Carrs' today! Aunt Mary would not like that.

With a sick feeling, Sam turned to go back in the house. All the Grantham kids were watching at various windows.

Help, she thought. Oh, Dad, help.

The questions came thick and fast once Sam entered the house. Aunt Mary started it. Sam could not help laughing to herself when she saw that Aunt Mary, who had taken her in without once checking to see if she had the right child, was curious about Alex now—Alex, who was the kid she was supposed to have had from the start.

She was glad the light in the hall was dim so they could not see how hard she had to struggle not to burst into giggles. Remembering Bilbo's peril and Mr. Carr's coma sobered her again.

"I could phone Mrs. Trueblood and ask but I don't like to do that," Aunt Mary was fussing. "But your mother ..."

"Mum met Sam at the airport," Sam lied. "We got there early. You know how you have to get there early. And she said we could be friends once we arrived. She's only here for the summer, just like me."

She bit off the flow of words, afraid she would make a glaring error any second. Maybe she had already.

Bethany was staring at her in a strange way.

"You talk in your sleep, did you know?" she asked.

Sam went rigid. She did know, as a matter of fact. Her father had teased her about it sometimes. She had done it a lot when she was little. Nowadays, she usually did it only when she was worried about something. She had plenty to worry her these days. Why hadn't she thought of that?

Josie was jumping up and down, her big eyes bright with curiosity.

"What does she say?" she demanded. "Tell us, tell us, tell us. Come on, Bethie."

"Don't call me Bethie," Bethany yelled at her.

"That's enough, girls. Bethany, go and have a bath. You smell like a horse. And don't bother Alex about whatever you may have heard her saying. You probably heard nothing but mumbling. That's what you do yourself. We'll talk about the boy later, dear. I think I will call the Truebloods. Maybe they'd like to come over for dinner."

Bethany was flouncing up the stairs. She turned her head for a parting shot.

"Ask her who David is," she said, her eyes filled with malice. "She says, 'I need you, David.' And she did not mumble, Mum. She spoke as clearly as me."

"As I," her mother corrected automatically.

One giggle escaped Sam. David was her father's name. She often called him David, especially when they were teasing each other. How she needed him!

"Can we eat?" Kenneth asked, ignoring his sister. "I'm starving, Mum. My backbone is poking out through my belly button."

Even Bethany choked down a laugh. Thomas went up to Kenneth and tried to peek up under his baggy sweatshirt. Josie spun around, shrieking with mirth. It did the trick. Mary Grantham, loving food herself, could not hear of a hungry child without springing to provide sustenance.

In two minutes, the hall had cleared except for Sam and Thomas and Kenneth. Kenneth's eyes met Sam's. There was no need for words. She saluted. He bowed. Thomas went on gazing at his brother's middle. When Kenneth followed his mother to the kitchen, Sam spoke softly to the small boy.

"Thomas, where would you hide a talking parrot?"

"In my toy basket," Thomas said immediately. "Would you like to borrow it?"

Sam remembered the basket with hope flooding into her heart.

"It might be just the thing," she whispered. "Can I really take it for a little while?"

"Come," Thomas said and trundled away ahead of her.

16

*I*n no time, Sam had the large empty basket clutched in her two hands. Where could she hide it until after dark?

"I'll hide it for you," Thomas said, "if you promise to tell me why later."

"I'll tell," Sam promised.

"Put it back behind the shoes in my closet," the little boy said, pointing. "They won't look there. I used to play it was my magic kingdom in there. Nobody goes in. I don't play that now but I haven't told them in case I need a place to myself. Who's David?"

"My dad," Sam said with a grin. "I needed help, you see. I thought you were too small. I was so wrong."

"I am small," Thomas told her seriously, "but I am helpful. Now let us go and see what they're all doing."

Right after supper, Alex paced up and down in front of the Truebloods'. She was waiting for the first sign of twilight, for the first sight of Sam and, nervously, for a car containing Mr. Carr's nephew.

Thank goodness Margaret was busy grooming dogs and waiting for someone coming to look at Sweet William, and Mr. Trueblood was busy at the store. They were wonderful at minding their own business, much better than the people Sam had ended up with. Mrs. Grantham had a way of looking at you as though she was not sure she should trust you.

"I'm here," Sam called, bumping up the road pulling a wagon with a large lidded basket on it. She was red-faced and out of breath.

Alex's eyes lit up. It was perfect. Now all she had to do was tell her about the hiding place she had discovered.

"That is just right," she began. "He'll love it."

"No, he won't," Sam said. "You have to put him into it, not me. He's going to be mad as a wet ... parrot."

"I don't think so," Alex said, grinning. "He'll just start eating it. He loves chewing on wood. I hope it isn't a basket you care about."

"It belongs to Thomas but he said he didn't care if it got damaged. I had to swear to introduce him to our bird sometime soon, though."

"You told him?" Alex gave her a shocked glance. "You promised ..."

Sam glared at her. She had gone to all this trouble and now Alex was going to have a purple fit about Thomas.

"You would have told, too, to get the basket," she snapped. "He's really little and he's good at keeping secrets. Let's move Bilbo and not stand around jabbering. Where are we putting him?"

Alex stared at her, shocked by Sam's outburst. But then she put it aside and just looked nervous.

"You better come and see," she said. "I looked for a better place but I couldn't think of anything."

"Shall we get Bilbo now before it gets darker?" Sam said. Her voice was unsteady but she did her level best to appear fearless.

Alex took a deep breath. Then she led the way. She had a towel tied around her waist as though she planned to start by giving the parrot a bath. She looked more anxious with every step. Bilbo Baggins began yelling at them the minute they came into the basement room.

"Hi, hi, hello and goodbye. No crackers, please. Hello, Bilbo, you old sweetie."

They approached his cage slowly. Neither of them wanted to alarm him. As they both returned his greeting, Sam noticed willow branches in the cage that had not been there last time she had visited. Clearly Bilbo had been enjoying chomping on them.

"They should have called you Beaver," she told the parrot.

He cocked his head to one side and made the sound of a telephone ringing.

"Get the basket," Alex said.

Sam opened her mouth to ask who had made Alex the boss. Then, glimpsing the other girl biting her lip, she relented. She wondered how Alex was going to manage transferring the bird from cage to basket, and then she decided to wait and see. She fetched the basket without uttering a word but her eyes were filled with questions. Alex was breathing fast when Sam got back, and she had untied the towel.

"Open the cage door, Sam," she ordered like a general commanding her troops.

Silently, Sam undid the main catch and swung the front down so that it made a shelf. Bilbo hopped out instantly. He had one eye fastened on Alex.

Alex climbed up on the closest chair and reached out her arms with the towel spread between her hands.

"Okay, boy," she began quietly. "Easy does it."

Wings whirred and flapped. To Sam, it seemed that at least three birds went whizzing right over her head. Then, to her astonished delight, she found Bilbo Baggins was on her shoulder, clinging to her shirt.

"Hey!" she breathed, wishing she had on a thicker shirt since his claws were digging into her shoulder.

"How will we ever do it?" Alex wailed, letting the towel flop down against her legs.

Sam did not know what possessed her. Slowly, with Bilbo digging his toenails in deeply, she sank down into a squatting position right next to Thomas's basket. Bilbo beat his wings around her ears in a wild flutter but did not move his feet.

Suddenly Alex swooped down with her towel spread out and, next thing, she had hold of one extremely agitated bird. With great care, she lifted the frantic bundle off Sam and down into the basket.

"Don't let go," Sam gasped, scrambling over to where the domed lid waited.

How they did it neither of them could have told later but, in two minutes flat, one African Grey parrot sat sulking inside a lidded basket.

"Hell," Bilbo said clearly. "Bloody hell."

"Is he saying 'Hello'?" Sam asked.

"I don't think so," Alex answered with a wobbly grin. Then she collapsed onto the floor.

"Oh, I was so afraid he was going to escape," she said.

"Yeah!" Sam returned, mopping her forehead. "Alex, we've got to hurry or that man might turn up. Where are we taking him?"

Sam's words yanked Alex onto her feet once more.

"Grab that end and follow me," she ordered.

Sam, tired of being bossed around, was about to protest when she realized that she had no idea where they were going. Out of the cottage they marched, across the yard to the farthest corner. There was a garden shed there but Sam knew that would not do. Then she remembered their tent, which was still pitched right behind it.

The three of them rounded the shed and there it was— Bilbo's temporary hideout, the tent.

"Oh, my!" Sam said, admiring and dismayed. "I forgot about it. Do you think it will work?"

Alex nodded vigorously although her eyes were anxious. Sam thought of something comforting.

"You know what? I think there's a smaller cage in Mr. C.'s basement. It might fit in there," said Alex.

"I think you're right. If it will, it'll be good. But, Alex ..."

"I know," Alex said. Her voice sounded miserable in the darkness. "Would your dad let you keep him?"

Sam felt sick at heart. She knew Alex loved Bilbo more than she did and she also knew that Alex's stepfather and her beige mother would never go for a parrot. Her father might but he worked at home. He said he needed quiet. Bilbo was not one bit quiet.

The angry parrot tried clapping his wings inside the basket and they struck hard against the wicker.

"Come on," Alex said. "We can't leave him in that."

They went back and found the smaller cage. Even though it was small enough, it was still heavy and awkward, and they finally used the wagon to haul it. It seemed to take hours. The lights shone out through the back windows of the Truebloods' house but nobody came out to investigate.

"They're all old," Alex said, thinking of the people in the nearby scatter of houses. "They watch TV, I think, and the Truebloods read." And yet …

At last, Bilbo, beady-eyed and ruffled and not one bit friendly, was settled with water in the water dish and food in the food container. Sam put in some walnuts she had taken from Aunt Mary's baking supplies. They already knew that Bilbo loved walnuts, the shells of which had been slightly cracked but not removed. He removed them with gusto.

"I have to get back," Sam said. "I'm already in trouble. They think you might be dangerous. When they find out the truth, they're going to go up in smoke."

"Maybe we can work it so they'll never have to know," Alex said.

But her voice held faint hope, and Sam knew it was only a matter of time. She told Alex about talking in her sleep.

"Just don't say, 'Alex, let's swap summers,'" Alex said.

Their long minutes of tension erupted into a burst of giggles, smothered with quick hands.

"If only I didn't have to share with Bethany," Sam said. "She's suspicious about me, I can tell, but she can't figure out what's going on. I guess your mother didn't tell them anything much." Sam picked up the wagon handle. "Well, good luck." She turned to leave, then stopped. "Wait a minute! Did you ask Mrs. T. about that envelope?"

Alex stared at her.

"I can't believe I forgot," she admitted. "I'll ask."

"Don't get your knickers in a knot over it," Sam told her. "Keep looking after our feathered friend. I wish we could get the big cage over."

"Yeah," Alex said in the darkness. "As Bilbo would say, 'Hell.'"

"Bloody hell," Sam laughed.

She set out, dragging the empty wagon. They had decided to leave the basket in the shed, just in case Bilbo had to be shifted again.

Maybe nobody had noticed it was late. Maybe nobody was worried. Maybe her name was not Sam.

17

When Sam got home, only Kenneth and Josie were there. Thomas had been knocked over by a boy on a motorbike and his mother and Bethany had taken him to the hospital. Not even Kenneth showed any curiosity about where Sam had been. They were far too worried about Thomas.

It was after ten when they brought the small boy home, his head bandaged.

"I had four stitches and I was as brave as a tiger," the wounded boy announced. Then he yawned and leaned against his mother.

"Hail the conquering hero comes," Kenneth said.

But Thomas was too tired and shaken to laugh.

The next morning Sam actually got up early enough to ride Echo when Aunt Mary was checking out the horses first thing. It was fun to walk, trot, and even canter without Bethany's critical eyes sizing up how she was progressing. That cool glance of the older girl brought out Sam's awkward side, which vanished whenever Bethany did.

When Bethany did arrive, she insisted that Sam canter. How had she guessed that Sam was nervous about cantering? Sam found her stomach squirming with fear the moment she started to follow Bethany's orders.

When Echo swung around a curve, Sam came close to sliding off, and she pulled the horse back to a sedate trot in spite of Bethany's scornful glance.

She wouldn't look so crabby if I weren't getting good, Sam told herself, knowing it was true.

She dismounted, rubbed Echo down, put away her tack, and headed for the house.

She and Alex had decided she had better not head for the Truebloods' until after lunch so any suspicion would quiet down, but waiting was a pain.

"Poor old Bilbo needs to adjust. I'll go sit with him," Alex had promised. "I'll check to see when the nephew comes too."

She had sounded smug, but so what? She didn't get to ride Echo.

Sam was eager to go and learn the latest but first she looked out for the mail delivery. There might be a postcard from Australia to take along.

To her surprise, Alex got a really fat letter this time. Sam was just going to stuff the letter into her jeans pocket, when Aunt Mary stopped her cold.

"I got a card from your mother myself," she said, sounding very serious and strangely sympathetic. "She asked me to stay with you while you read her letter. Could you read it right away because I have some riding lessons to give in an hour."

Sam wanted to refuse. She had no business reading Alex's mail, after all. But she could not come up with a good excuse.

The very first paragraph hit her like a boot in the kneecap.

Alex darling, we've a big surprise for you. I'm going to tell you right off the bat and I hope, once you are over the shock, you'll be as pleased as we both are. We have decided to sell up in Canada and emigrate to Australia. A friend of Perry's has invited him to join him in his clinic. Perry says he'd have to be crazy to pass up such an opportunity. We love the climate here and we have already made friends who are going to help us get the papers we need. We have made a bid on a house in the community where all the clinic staff lives. Alex, we have more big news to tell you. You will be so excited, I hope. You won't believe this at first. I didn't when the doctor

*told me in May. You are going to have a baby brother or
sister. You used to ask for a little sister when your dad
was with us. Do you remember? I hope you are pleased.
Perry is tickled pink. We want our baby to be born here
in Sydney, so he or she will have dual citizenship.*

*I hope you are sitting down, sweetheart, because this
must all come as a big shock—but I think you are going
to love it here as much as we do.*

*You must have learned to love horses by this time and
you can ride here to your heart's content. Our friends go
to the races.*

Sam choked down a spurt of laughter. Then she backed
up and sank down onto a kitchen chair. She thought she
might be sick. Poor Alex! Aunt Mary opened her mouth but
Sam bent her head over the next page and kept reading.

*Just think, next Christmas you can go swimming
instead of having to shovel snow.*

*The doctor says the baby might be twins. I guess I
should have said something before we left but I could
not until I felt clearer about our future. Now Perry and
I have got everything settled and he has found he could
not be happier about the working conditions.*

*Write soon. I want to phone you but Perry thinks
that long distance costs too much, and anyway we*

should give you a chance to get adjusted to the news first. Besides, it always seems the wrong time of day and we are busy sight-seeing before I get too far along to want to drive long distances. There are lots of good libraries …

love, Mum

Sam looked up, her expression dazed, her eyes wide. Aunt Mary patted her shoulder comfortingly and gazed at her white face with enormous sympathy.

She thinks she understands, Sam thought, choking down a burst of hysterical giggles. She probably thinks I'm jealous. She has no notion she's comforting the wrong kid.

"It's a big shock, I know. Your mother is shocked herself, I think," Mary Grantham said gently. "But it will be nice for you not being an only child any longer. And I'll bet you just love living Down Under."

"I … yes, it will be…. I mean, it is a shock," Sam mumbled, folding the pages up and stuffing them back into the envelope. "Aunt Mary, can I go out for a walk? I need to think."

"Of course," Aunt Mary said. "But don't stay away too long. We can talk more when you come home."

Home, Sam thought wildly. It isn't home. It isn't Alex's home either. How could Alex's mother write to her like that?

She should have told her before they left … and she could have phoned, whatever that Perry said.

She practically ran out the door. She leaped onto Kenneth's old bike without asking leave and took off at top speed. Poor Alex! She was going to hate it.

As she pulled away, she heard Aunt Mary calling something after her.

"She says she wrote to tell your dad too."

That was what she was shouting. What on earth was Alex's dad supposed to do? Sam knew Alex loved her father more than she loved her mother. Well, maybe not loved him more but felt more at home and easy with him. Maybe, just maybe, her father could help out somehow.

At the Truebloods', she tumbled off the bike and, bypassing the house, headed for Bilbo Baggins's hiding place. Then she saw two things that stopped her. Alex was standing half-hidden by a big tree watching the Carrs' cottage, and a strange car was in the driveway.

Sam slipped along the fence, watching the windows of the cottage. No face peered out at her. As she came level with Alex's tree, Alex reached out, grabbed her elbow, and yanked her out of sight of the windows.

"It's him, Mr. Carr's nephew. He's been over to the Truebloods' place. He went into their house about half an hour ago and I haven't heard a sound out of him."

"How's Bilbo?" Sam demanded.

"He's fine but, oh Sam, he's loose in there. I had him out of the cage when the car came and I couldn't make him go back in. I had to leave him loose but he's zipped in and he seems quiet. What'll we do?"

Sam opened her mouth to say she had no notion and why were they whispering? Then she remembered the letter. Recalling it was like having an icicle fall on her head. She survived but felt stunned.

She reached for the envelope in her pocket and pulled her hand away. This was not the time. Yet she would hate it if the other girl was handed a letter meant for her and chose not to pass it over until she thought Sam was in the right mood.

"A letter came from your mother," she muttered. "Aunt Mary gave it to me ..."

"Not now," Alex said, her voice sharp, her eyes never leaving the sidewalk leading from Margaret's front door to Mr. Carr's. "Watch out for him."

"There he is," Sam squeaked, feeling her heart beginning to rattle her ribs. Both girls held their breath and stared, goggle-eyed, at the man who was striding toward the cottage door.

18

He disappeared. Sam opened her mouth to speak when the back door opened and the same man stood looking out at the garden. "He looks like a …" Sam started to whisper.

"A rat," Alex breathed.

Sam saw what she meant but it was just his yellow buck teeth. The rest of him was ordinary, just a thin middle-aged man in a rumpled suit. He stood there, staring all around. Then he began to stroll down the garden path, heading right for the tree behind which they were sheltering.

Not sheltering. Trapped.

Sam could not stand there, waiting to be caught. She ducked away from Alex's clutching hand and, entirely forgetting the parrot, hunched over and ran to hide in the tent. She unzipped the door and got one foot inside. Then an angry whir of flapping African Grey feathers beat up into her face. She screamed and toppled over backwards.

"Help!" she yelled, as Bilbo escaped and took off. He flew lopsidedly but fast toward the cottage.

"Don't, Bilbo," she heard Alex moan.

As the parrot swerved through the air toward his old home, the man spun around and ran for the same sanctuary. Bilbo, alarmed, did an about-face and lighted on the back of old Mr. Carr's lawn chair. The chair was made of aluminum, and it rocked under the unexpected weight of the frightened bird. Bilbo gave a truly deafening shriek and, to Sam's astonishment, the man in the house screamed almost as loudly.

Then he thrust up the kitchen window and bellowed at them: "I'm calling the Humane Society. Don't go near that bird. He's vicious."

He slammed down the window.

Alex held her breath and started to walk slowly and quietly to the parrot's perch but Bilbo did not wait for her. Perhaps he understood the threats Mr. Carr's nephew had yelled. Perhaps he was drunk on freedom. But, just as Alex drew within arm's reach, the parrot spread his wings and flew up into a nearby tree and sat high above them, peering down. To Alex, he looked petrified. To Sam, he looked smug.

Whichever it was, he was clearly not about to return to them. Not without some powerful incentive.

"Holy smoke!" Sam gasped and ran to stand beside Alex, under the tree the parrot had chosen.

"I might be able to coax him down," Alex faltered.

The window was raised once more.

"They're coming in ten minutes," the man shouted. "Children, don't go near that bird. He bites. He is truly vicious. Believe me, I have scars to prove it."

The girls ignored him. Alex had begun to climb. Talking softly to soothe her friend, she had managed to get onto the lowest branch. Sam spotted Kenneth's swimming towel in the bicycle basket and ran to get it.

"Here, Alex," she called softly, tossing it up to her.

"I'm not fooling," Mr. Carr's nephew called again. "Girl, don't get near him."

Bilbo hopped up to a higher branch and turned his head sideways so he could keep an eye on Alex.

"Hurry up, George," Bilbo yelled suddenly. He sounded worried but not lethal.

Sam turned to the frantic man. The time had come to start talking or Alex would lose her bird for sure.

"My friend knows this bird well," she said. "Your uncle told her she could keep Bilbo, actually. He said he had left instructions with a friend. He really did say Alex …"

"Oh, you can have him. Believe me, you are more than welcome to him. I can't imagine anyone in his right mind wanting such a nasty creature. My uncle left instructions with the lady next door. I've just spoken to her. She has mislaid the envelope but she's looking for it. I get the house, I believe; you get the bird."

Suddenly Margaret Trueblood was hurrying across the grass with the envelope clutched in her hand.

"I found it," she puffed. "I haven't had a chance to speak to the girls yet."

She turned to look up at Alex, still perched on her branch.

"Sam, Mr. Carr died this afternoon. He had a second stroke. He gave me this letter a couple of weeks ago. I don't know what it is about but I'm to give it to his lawyer."

Alex did not move or speak. She did not even look down. After a long silence, she moved up to the next branch.

"I'll tell them at the Humane Society not to come if you think you can manage that creature," the man said.

Sam watched Alex, wishing she would say something. But when she did speak, it was to the bird.

"Don't worry, Bilbo. Nobody will hurt you. Come on and let me lift you down," Alex murmured. "I'll give you walnuts."

Sam wondered if her friend had heard what Margaret had said. She appeared to be utterly concentrating on getting her parrot to safety. Maybe she hadn't heard.

Then as Alex drew level with Bilbo, he plucked her glasses off her face. He was instantly fascinated with them and so pleased to have snagged them that Alex actually got him to "step up" onto her hand and then her shoulder. Slowly, slowly, she began to inch downward again. Bilbo almost dropped the spectacles but, as they swung in his beak, he stopped to look down at them. Alex and Sam between them wrapped him up in Kenneth's towel. Sam was ready for just about anything but the parrot seemed relieved to be caught. He had never lived in the wild and, grand as it was, it was also too big and strange for him. He dropped the glasses and pecked Alex's earlobe in a friendly fashion.

"Good old Bilbo," Alex crooned, stepping onto solid ground.

Then Sam saw the tears running down her friend's face and, without a word, ran to pick up the glasses.

As Sam hooked them onto her friend's ears and Alex's fuzzy world grew clear again, Alex remembered doing the same thing for Mr. Carr at the beginning of the summer and felt the lump in her throat grow twice as big. He had given her more than a parrot. With him, after the first couple of days, she had been able to be herself and not worry about pretending she was someone else. Recalling that moment when she had pulled him out of the rose bush, she realized that she would never see him again.

She longed to run away from Sam and Margaret and Mr. Carr and even Bilbo and throw herself on her bed and give in to her grief.

But this was not the time. Bilbo did not know he had lost his old friend. He needed his new one. Poor Bilbo. He began to scramble up her shirt.

Alex pushed her pain away and moved carefully toward the cage.

"Come inside, when you've gotten him safely caged. We can make arrangements to have your parents pick him up," the man said.

"Before you talk to him," Sam blurted out to Alex, feeling doubly wretched, "you must read your mother's letter. I'm sorry but you have to."

"Not now," Alex answered in the toneless voice of a computer, but she took the letter and jammed it into her back pocket.

Bilbo was now in the tent. But instead of going to Mr. Carr's house, Alex went across the lawn and into the Truebloods, leaving her friend and Mr. Carr's nephew staring after her. Margaret Trueblood gazed at the girl vanishing into the house and followed her indoors, without wasting a glance on Sam or Mr. Carr's jittery nephew. She, too, had seen the tears on Alex's face and the blind look in her eyes.

19

*A*lex sat on the edge of her bed and replayed the nephew's last words. She could not let herself think about her friend's death right now. He was gone where she could not reach him. Bilbo still needed her. She had to move him. "Your parents," he had said. She had never once thought that far ahead. Where on earth could she take a parrot? Not just *a* parrot … her parrot.

She had thought about where to hide Bilbo temporarily but had not thought ahead about where to take him if Mr. Carr's nephew handed him over. She began to rock back and forth, trying to comfort herself and get her tumbling thoughts in focus.

Mum, she thought desperately. Perry. Never in a million years would they help her out.

The man had looked confused. She had seen that much before she walked off. Alex did not blame him. She felt she had been confused ever since she and Sam had come up with their goofy plan.

Sam came running up the stairs. She peered at Alex and then looked away.

"Hey, it's late. I gotta go," she said. "Call me later when you've read that letter. I mean it. I won't be able to sleep if you don't."

Alex just sat, not answering. Sam shrugged and left, dragging her feet on the stairs. In the kitchen, Margaret Trueblood chatted to her faithful Button and heated some water for tea.

Alex looked down at Milkweed and Peony, who were dancing around her. Then she sank back, full-length, on the bed. The two papillons jumped up and pressed close, as though they guessed she needed their comforting presence. As she reached for them, her mother's envelope poked her in the back. Hardly noticing what she was doing, she pulled it out and stared at it.

The envelope had been opened. She scowled at it, confused. Then she understood. Sam must have been being watched. Otherwise she wouldn't have opened the letter. How strange! Alex slipped out the pages and glanced down at the top sheet.

Trying to concentrate her scattered thoughts, she

skimmed the first few lines and then slowed down. Even finding Bilbo had not given her such a stunning jolt.

"No," Alex whispered, scrunching up the letter in her two fists. "I won't go. She can't make me. I won't go and I won't be thrilled about any stupid baby. They can keep it instead of me and they'll be happy as clams. Dad … I'll have to find Dad. He'll stop it. He won't let them. It's kidnapping!"

For the first time in hours, Bilbo Baggins was forgotten. Alex turned over and buried her face in the pillows. Milkweed and Peony nosed at her heaving back, knowing she was in trouble, trying to help. Alex ignored them.

"Dad," she cried, "where are you? Oh, Dad, please, I need you so."

20

Sam whizzed back to Aunt Mary's wishing Alex had read the terrible letter before she left. The minute she got home, she would call. She charged up the walk and burst into the house only to be greeted by words that stopped her dead.

"Alex, your father has come to see you," Kenneth said. "When you weren't here, he went off to buy a newspaper. Mum's at a meeting at the church."

Sam gasped and dropped into the closest chair. Then a grin spread across her face. Alex loved her father so much and had missed him so much and wondered why he hadn't written. He must be one of the good guys. He would help the two of them sort it out.

But she must talk to him without the Grantham family sitting around listening.

"Kenneth," she said slowly, "when he gets here, I really want to talk to him in private. I mean ..."

"I know what you mean," Kenneth said. "Thomas is in bed and I'll keep the girls upstairs if I can. I think that must be his car now."

He jumped up and ran for the stairs. Sam got to her feet and faced the door.

Help, she thought. Help me.

Alex's father knocked and walked into the hall.

"I'm back," he called. "Is she home yet?"

Sam held her breath as footsteps approached the door. Then, just as Alex's father entered the living room and Sam opened her mouth to try to warn him, Josie came flying down the stairs like a human avalanche.

"I won't stay up there," she was shrieking. "I want to see him. Oh, Alex, is that really your daddy? Are you happy he's come?"

Sam walked across the living-room carpet as though she had on concrete shoes. The man in the doorway, who was staring blankly at her, looked so like Alex it was funny. He had the same thick glasses and the same grey-green eyes. But, if Sam didn't speak up, he was about to ruin everything.

"Hi, Dad," she said loudly, pointedly ignoring Josie's questions. "What a surprise! Let's go outside where we can talk in private."

He didn't bat an eye.

"Good thinking," Alex's father said. "You've changed so much I hardly recognized you. We certainly have some catching up to do. Zelda wrote to me but I gather she doesn't know the whole of it."

"No," Sam mumbled, going red. "She wrote to ... I read the letter she sent here."

"Aren't you going to give him a kiss?" Josie asked, shocked at their cool greeting.

"We're shy," the man said, grinning suddenly.

It was Alex's grin. Sam all at once felt hopeful that maybe everything would turn out right after all. Maybe.

She grabbed his hand and tugged him out the door. She closed it firmly on Josie, who was following like a puzzled puppy.

"How did you come?" she asked.

"How did ... Oh, in my Jeep."

"Then let's take it and go to Alex. She got that awful letter from her mother and she hadn't read it when I had to leave her and I think maybe your coming is some kind of miracle."

"That poor kid," Alex's father said. "You seem to know what Zelda wrote. Why did you read her letter?"

"Aunt Mary made me. Alex's mum said she was to sit with me ... Alex, I mean ... while she read it. So I had to. You see, she thinks I'm Alex. I mean, Aunt Mary ..."

"Which way?" Mr. Kennedy asked grimly, turning the key in the ignition.

Sam felt crushed. Gulping down a sob that all at once threatened to burst out of her, she told him which way to go. Neither of them spoke as the Jeep roared up the road.

"This is it," Sam said, pointing to the Truebloods' house. "And I think Alex's mother is awful! She said she didn't phone because it would cost too much money. Perry told her not to and she did what he said."

"Good old Zelda," the man said, parking the Jeep in the driveway. "I know what you mean, I'm not too crazy about her myself. But she broke the custody agreement, moving without telling me and then leaving the country. She may have cooked her goose."

Sam had no idea what he was talking about. She sprang out of the Jeep and ran for the house without waiting.

"Alex!" she yelled. "Alex!"

Margaret was putting on the kettle, about to take a cup of tea to the sobbing girl upstairs.

"Hello, Alex," she called. "Sam's in her room."

"I know," Sam said. "But I've brought her a visitor who will fix everything. We'll be down in a few minutes."

She knew it was not polite but she wanted to get Alex and her father together without wasting one second and, also, she wanted Alex to do the introducing. After all, she did not really know this father. She raced up the stairs and flung open Alex's door. Her friend was lying face down on the bed. She raised her head and turned a tear-blinded face toward her co-conspirator. The look she shot at her was one of pure fury.

"You might have warned me ..." she started to yell.

Then she caught sight of Sam's companion. Even without her glasses, she knew ... she knew who that shadow belonged to. But it couldn't be. For an instant, she stayed frozen in place, her eyes round with shock. Then she reached out and snatched up her glasses and jammed them on her face.

Sam knew she should leave at once but she found that she, like Josie, wanted to witness this historic moment!

Alex gasped, sprang up, and flew across the space to the waiting man whose arms were open to catch her. Then the two of them were hugging so tight Sam was sure there would be some cracked ribs.

"Come on down when you're ready," she said and backed out fast, shutting the door behind her.

She stood hesitating for a moment, took a step toward the stairs, stopped, and then moved to sit on the top step and wait for future developments. This had turned out to be an unpredictable day. She did not believe she had had one to match it since ... since she had sat beside Alex Kennedy on an airplane.

Suddenly, in the middle of a chuckle, she remembered the African Grey parrot in the garden. Holy catfish! Where were they at with Bilbo Baggins? Nothing had been settled when she had left for the Granthams'.

"Are you all right, Bilbo?" she whispered.

But she could not keep her mind on him. She was trying to eavesdrop on Alex. Was she crying? Or could she possibly be laughing? Was there some way Mr. Kennedy could solve everything? She could not imagine how.

But nothing could surprise me, she murmured. Today I'm ready for anything.

But she was wrong. Margaret Trueblood came to the foot of the stairs and smiled up at her.

"Hello," she said. "Am I right in believing that you are the real Sam?"

21

*T*he … the real Sam?" Sam faltered.

As she stared down at the woman, it came back to her. She had burst into the house shouting "Alex … Alex!" After all these weeks, she had blown the whole thing in a single second.

"Wait right there," Margaret Trueblood said with a broad smile. She came back with a photograph album.

"How would you like to see a picture of Sam's mother?" she said.

Feeling strangely breathless, Sam slid her bottom down the stairs and held out her hands. The album was already open to the page.

Sam, struggling to clear her muddled thoughts, stared down at a picture of herself. But it was one she did not recognize. The girl in the photo had the face she herself saw every time she looked in the mirror but her hair was straight and she had on an old-fashioned blouse and skirt Sam had never seen.

"Who ..." she whispered.

"Her name was Cecily Alcott before she married," Margaret Trueblood said gently. "She's Samantha Scott's mother. The other day, I found an old album and I thought I'd show Sam what her grandmother and I looked like when we were her age. But when I came on a picture of her grandmother with her daughter Cecily, it wasn't my Sam's face I saw looking back at me. It was her friend Alex's. Turn the page."

Sam stared at the two pictures on the following page. The first was of two teenagers. One must be Mrs. Trueblood, the other one Grandma. And a newer snapshot was pasted next to it. Underneath it was written "Cecily Scott and her newborn daughter Samantha."

"You have to be Sam," the woman said very gently. "I don't know why ..."

She let her words hang in the air but her eyes were kind.

There was a long moment of utter silence.

"Alex is afraid of horses," Sam finally managed to get out through stiff lips. "And she loves to read. And Dad couldn't afford ... I never had a chance to ride.... If we switched, she could read and I could ride."

"It makes perfect sense," Margaret Trueblood said, her voice dry but her lips twitching. Sam felt her cheeks redden.

Her eyes dropped back to the book she was holding. Automatically her hands turned the next page in the old album. Then her gaze was riveted on the next picture of Cecily.

This time the girl was sulky but she, too, looked familiar. A smile tugged at the corners of Sam's mouth. All at once, for perhaps the first time, her mother became not a shut-away memory of her dad's but a girl like herself, someone she would have loved, someone who would have loved her.

"Someone who did love me," she whispered. She had known her mother for a little while, eighteen months before the car crash. This girl, grown up, must have held her and rocked her and even told her stories.

In the last picture, Cecily was a woman. She was in her early twenties, Sam guessed, and her hair was combed properly and she looked happy and pretty and less like Sam but still the lump in Sam's throat doubled in size.

Then Alex and her father came out into the upstairs hall.

"Sam, it's my father," Alex announced in a voice that sang like a bird at dawn. "He's going to try to fix everything."

"That'll take some doing," Margaret Trueblood said, reaching to pull Sam to her feet. "We'll all need to talk. I'm Margaret Trueblood, by the way."

She stretched out her hand to Mr. Kennedy.

"Jonathan Kennedy," he said, shaking the hand and grinning at her. "But everyone calls me Jon."

They headed into the living room as Mrs. Trueblood went on talking.

"Well, I've had my suspicions for quite a while and, once I unearthed the album Sam is hugging to her chest, I was sure. I was not sure what I should do since their scheme seemed to be running so smoothly. So I waited for fate to take a hand."

"Am I fate?" Jonathan Kennedy asked. "I suppose I am. Or maybe Zelda is. She finally sent me an address where she believed Alex was spending the summer. 'In case of an emergency,' she said. There was no emergency except I wanted to see my daughter and, lo and behold, we were within driving distance of each other. But the address led me to Sam, and now Alex. I hadn't heard from my child in a while and I was beginning to wonder if she was mad at me about something or just too busy having a wonderful summer to write to me. I was sending my letters to Zelda's old apartment and she hadn't made any arrangement to have mail sent on."

"Oh," Alex said, understanding everything. "She was so busy planning stuff …"

"Never mind her. Now I want to hear the story from the start, including your acquiring an exotic pet."

"Bilbo! Alex, we've got to check on Bilbo!" Sam cried.

"Yeah," Alex agreed, stumbling over her feet in her rush to get up.

Margaret Trueblood rose and held onto Alex's shoulder for a moment.

"Good idea. The poor man has called twice. He wants someone to save him from the winged menace," she said. "Such a fuss about a parrot."

Alex pulled away and ran after Sam. Behind her, she heard her father saying, "A parrot!"

Side by side, without exchanging a word, the girls dashed across the grass to the tent. Alex pulled up the zipper. The cage door was ajar and she saw no African Grey parrot.

"Oh, no!" Sam yelped. "Not again!"

Alex laughed.

"Look down, Sam," she said. "And keep your feet together."

Bilbo was standing right in front of her feet, his head ducking to snap at her curly shoelaces. She had on the rainbow ones Dad had given her for her birthday. They were out of style but she had not told him. Bilbo clearly thought they were superb.

Alex gave the parrot a stern look that Bilbo did not see.

"You cannot keep doing this to us," she scolded. "Shoo! Into your cage, birdbrain."

She clapped her hands as hard as she could as she spoke. Bilbo, taken off guard and alarmed, flapped and banged and somehow was back in the safe shelter of his cage. He perched on the swing and glared at her. Alex shut the door fast.

"The catch is bent," she said, fiddling with it. "There, that should hold for a while."

"Let's see him," Alex's father's voice said. He ducked his head down level with theirs.

"An African Grey, as I live and breathe! Handsome," he said. "You will love my new friend."

Sam and Alex both jerked around. Alex looked shocked but did not speak. Sam spoke for the two of them.

"What new friend?" she asked.

Alex's father straightened up and grinned at them.

"Don't get your knickers in a knot," he said. "I promise you'll love her. She's not a bit threatening. She's my dear companion."

Sam and Alex did not look at each other. They felt as though a tremor had shaken the ground beneath their feet. Adults could not be trusted. The girls would wait and see. And, while they were waiting, they would be filled not with eager anticipation but with uneasy dread.

"Jon, bring that poor bird into the pantry," Mrs. Trueblood called as they were about to go back to the house. "The dogs can't get in there and there's a wide shelf you can stand the cage on. I remember him now. Joanna Carr was very fond of him, but George never mentioned him and I thought he had died."

Mr. Kennedy eased the bulky cage through the tent flap, with Bilbo still inside, and lugged it to the house. He had to put it down once to rest. Bilbo peered out at them as though they were kidnapping bandits. But once they put fresh water in his water dish and added some walnuts and peanuts to his food, he calmed down.

Then Margaret Trueblood took a weight off Sam's heart by announcing that she had phoned Aunt Mary and gotten permission for Sam to sleep over.

"I said you were upset about a letter your mother had sent you and she was very understanding," she said. "While I was at it, I invited the entire clan for a supper barbecue tomorrow. Daniel will be thrilled. He likes cooking out-of-doors but I don't. It's perfect timing because Duncan Grantham comes home from Manitoba late tonight. That'll help cushion the shock."

"I can get a room at the Holiday Inn," Alex's dad started to say.

"You'll do no such thing. We have a perfectly good guest room going to waste. The girls can make your bed for you. I want you on the spot tomorrow. We're lucky that it's Sunday so nobody has to be at work—even Daniel. It won't be easy for Mary. Humour is not her strong suit."

Alex, remembering how anxious Mrs. Trueblood had been about the new puppies the day she herself had arrived, was surprised she was inviting people over.

"Josie and Thomas will want to play with the dogs," she said.

"And they can. Are you thinking of the day Tansy had her pups and how we had to be so careful around them? They are seven weeks old tomorrow, and anyway we can put them upstairs. They can play with the older ones to their hearts' content. And you can take them to visit the babies. They understand about newborn animals, you know. They have foals born over there."

Sam nodded. Her eyes grew dreamy remembering when one of the mares was having her spindly-legged baby. Sam had been taken out, as soon as it was safe, to see the tiny filly, still damp and tottering. She was grateful that Alex's mother had not written before that birth.

Daniel Trueblood came in just in time to hear the two girls taking turns relating all the ups and downs of their plot. The adults tried to appear outraged but kept breaking into laughter.

"It's kind of like that old movie *The Parent Trap*," Alex said at one point.

"I think I'd better be the one to tell Mary Grantham," Mrs. Trueblood said finally. "This is one of the most confusing stories I've ever heard. I see how it happened but even so …"

"I'm sorry, but thank you. I've been dreading telling," Sam said, heaving a sigh of relief.

"Oh, but you're going to be standing at my side. Both of you. I'll do the talking but you'll have to take whatever comes next."

"I guess I'm sorry we were dishonest," Alex chimed in softly. "I'm still glad we did it, though. I've got Sam for my friend. I've got my father back and Bilbo for my lifelong companion. They can live to be eighty, you know."

Her father gave her a funny look.

Sam, watching him, saw his mouth quirk up at one corner but he did not say why and she was too polite to ask.

Sam never forgot the expressions on the faces of the Grantham family when Margaret Trueblood broke the news to them the next afternoon.

"So," she finished up, smiling at them all, "I'm afraid your Alex is really my Sam and my Sam should have been your Alex—except her father is going to steal her from both of us."

Bethany reared back as though she had discovered Sam was a spy. Kenneth kept struggling not to laugh. Josie went on and on asking bewildered questions that everyone ignored. Thomas just smiled to himself. And Mary Grantham kept saying to Sam, "But your mother, Alex. Your poor mother!"

Sam felt so guilty she could hardly answer.

"I'm Sam," she said. "Samantha Scott. I don't have a mother."

Mary Grantham looked as mixed-up as Josie.

"Her mother died when she was a baby and her name is really Samantha," Mrs. Trueblood said very slowly, as though she were talking to someone who did not understand English. "Alex lives with her mother and stepfather. They have decided to move to Australia and, if her father can talk her mother around, Alex will only go there for visits. She has had her daughter all to herself for the last few years and he thinks it is his turn."

"Why didn't he get custody?" Duncan Grantham asked gruffly. His tone betrayed that he felt sorry for his wife and annoyed by the girls who had tricked her and were going to get away with it.

Jonathan Kennedy grew red and got to his feet but Margaret Trueblood waved at him to sit down again.

"He didn't have a proper job at the time. He has one now. He's an artist, and he recently began teaching at a community college and a high school. He even has a dental plan. He was supposed to have visitation rights and Zelda was to keep him informed about any move. She didn't bother. I suppose, in her defence, she doubted he'd be able to come all the way to Vancouver to get Alex for weekends."

"I'm having trouble following all this," Mary Grantham said faintly. "Alex is really Sam?"

"You got it, Mum," Bethany said but she did not sound as impatient as usual. Clearly, she understood how her mother felt. Betrayed, lied to, tricked.

Then Sam fixed everything by saying sadly, "I just

wanted to ride horses. I never had a chance. I've loved horses ever since I can remember."

Her words worked like a magic wand. Bethany's scowl vanished and her mother smiled forgivingly at Samantha Scott, horsewoman.

"I was thinking just yesterday that it was a shame you had to go home before school starts. You've made such progress in your riding that we might have entered you in the Fergus Fall Fair."

Sam stared at her, unable to believe what she had just heard. Bethany grinned and did not look furious. Duncan Grantham turned away to hide a smile.

"I knew you weren't Alice a long time ago," Thomas said softly.

Everyone stared at him.

Josie rounded on him. "You did not," she yelled. "How could you, dummy?"

"How?" Sam said quickly.

"Your shoes," Thomas said. "They're like my school shoes. Your names are inside. I saw when we were by the river. Alice's shoes had a name beginning with *S* and Sam's had an *A*. They were wrong."

There was a stupefied silence. Then Duncan Grantham burst into a roar of laughter.

"Well done, my son," he said, tousling Thomas's hair. "One Grantham, at least, has his wits about him."

"The food's ready," Daniel Trueblood sang out. "Come and get it. Pick up a bun on your way and put whatever you want on it."

Alex and Sam stayed where they were for a long moment. They both felt limp. But it was over.

When everyone was full and the talk was flowing easily, the atmosphere was much less tense. Plans were made for Sam to fetch her things and move to the Truebloods'.

"But you can still come and ride," Bethany offered abruptly, without consulting her parents.

"She can't go until I see the bird, you know," Thomas said. "Sam promised because of my basket."

"What basket?" Mary Grantham said.

Sam let Margaret Trueblood explain while they took the Grantham kids to meet Bilbo and the puppies.

"Did you like my basket, Bilbo Baggins?" Thomas asked the parrot, his tone solemn, his eyes sparkling.

For once, Bilbo spoke up at exactly the right moment.

"Get along with you, you silly billy," he said, in Mrs. Carr's voice.

Thomas beamed and Sam felt pleased. Usually Bilbo listened when he was talked to and only responded when he was getting no attention.

The Granthams had to go home then to tend to the horses and put Thomas to bed. Sam went along so that she could get her belongings to take to the Trueblood house. As she started stuffing things into her duffle bag, the children, Bethany included, gathered to watch.

"This isn't your home now," Josie said sadly.

Sam's eyes stung with unshed tears at the lonesome note in Josie's voice. She bent down and gave the small girl a swift hug.

"I know," she said. "But I wasn't supposed to come here, you know. My grandmother sent me to stay with Margaret."

"We were just getting used to having you around," Bethany, said patting her forlorn little sister's shoulder. "She'll be back, Josie. She loves Echo too much to stay away."

"Well, you can have your friends to sleep over now," Sam said, looking under the bed for a missing sock.

"I guess ..." Bethany agreed, fondling the stuffed lamb that had been Sam's since babyhood.

Kenneth said, "Did you hear Thomas? He told Mum you're the best sister he has ever had."

They all laughed. Sam wished she could take Thomas home with her. Her father would so enjoy him.

Everything was still not settled that evening. It took three days. There were phone calls to Australia. Email messages flew back and forth. They were not supposed to hear about Alex's mother's reaction but Sam listened in on the upstairs phone. Alex's mother had been crying, and her husband the dentist had sounded huffy. But Sam guessed that they were not too upset. She breathed silently and strained not to miss a word. Then the papillons barked and gave her away.

"Hang up, please, Sam," Alex's father's voice said in her ear and she had to do as he asked but she had found out enough to comfort Alex.

"When your dad said he had a steady paycheque with a dental plan," Sam said, laughing, "your mother sounded flabbergasted."

Alex looked into the distance. Then she said quietly, "If he had done that in the first place, we'd probably still be together ... although maybe not. She used to say all she wanted was a sense of security."

Sam looked away from the sadness that fell across her friend's face like a shadow.

"Things change," she said uncomfortably. "My dad says you have to go with the changes or get stuck like cement."

Alex did not answer for a long moment. She took her glasses off and breathed on them. Then she polished them with the hem of her T-shirt.

"My dad says we're like plants. They grow or they wilt. You take your pick," Alex said finally.

"Easy for him to say," said Sam, glancing at her.

"Not all that easy," Alex said. "Anyway, I know we're still growing. I hear about it every time I need new shoes."

Sam laughed. Her feet were bigger than Alex's but she knew exactly what the other girl meant.

Finally everything was settled. The plan was that the next morning a small convoy would travel to Alex's new home. Mrs. Trueblood and Sam would drive in the van, which could hold the big birdcage, and Alex and her father would drive in his car, with Bilbo in the small cage. Then Mrs. Trueblood would bring Sam back for the last few days before she went home to Vancouver. That way Sam and Margaret could get to know each other better—and make an awkward phone call to Sam's grandmother.

"I'm glad you aren't going yet. We still have over a week of summer left," Kenneth said to Sam.

Sam shot him a startled glance. She had been so taken up with the mixed-up summer she and Alex had created, made ever more mixed-up by the coming of Bilbo, she had not thought much about what would happen after Alex went away.

"I love those little dogs," Kenneth finished.

Did he only want to stay friends because of Milkweed and Peony? Sam thought about getting mad and changed her mind. She liked the papillons herself. Maybe Margaret would let her name one the way Alex had named Sweet William.

22

When the morning came, Sam felt sad inside, knowing that the strange summer was ending. They had been unable to go to Mr. Carr's funeral because he had been cremated and his ashes had been taken to the village where he and his wife had lived when they were young. Although that added to her lonesome feeling, she and Alex were glad for him. They knew it was what he had wanted.

Alex's father lived in a small house near Lake Ontario. When they reached it, they all piled out. Alex was looking nervous. Sam sympathized. Thank goodness her dad had no "new friend" waiting to meet her.

They trooped up the steps to the porch.

"We can leave Bilbo out here for a moment," Alex's father said, grinning. "I wouldn't want him to bite my lady."

Alex thrust her right hand festooned with Band-Aids deep into her pocket.

"Bilbo wouldn't hurt a fly," she declared.

Her father unlocked the door and swung it wide.

"Hello, hello," called a woman's voice. "Step right in. Step right up."

If that's his friend, she sounds insane, Sam thought, her eyes meeting Alex's.

Then they walked into the big living room and saw the lady herself.

"Meet Jazz," said Alex's father, laughing at their astonished faces. "She's an African Grey. They're the best talkers, you know."

"A parrot! You mean she's a parrot!" the two girls shrieked.

The parrot, in a cage by the window, eyed them with a suspicious stare. She liked shrieking herself but she was not used to screeching human beings.

"Why didn't you tell us?" demanded Alex, her face shining with a mixture of relief and delight.

"I did say I had a new friend. I even mentioned a companion," he said. "I'm sure you've heard parrots called 'companion birds'? I met up with her in a pet shop. We both needed a friend, didn't we, Jazzy girl?"

"Dad, they can live to be eighty!" Alex exclaimed. "Aren't you a little old ..."

"Why do you think I've hooked up with you again?" her father teased, his eyes sparkling behind his thick glasses. "I had to find someone I could leave my parrot to. I knew I could count on my own flesh and blood to support me in my lunacy."

Alex broke into a peal of laughter.

"Wait till Mum hears!" she cried. "She always knew you were crazy."

When Jon Kennedy lugged both of Bilbo's cages into the house, Jazz and Bilbo glared at each other and instantly looked away. Then they looked again. They were not immediate buddies but they were clearly fascinated.

As Alex took her stuff into the room she was to have, Jazz yelled, "Goodbye, you old poop."

Alex dropped her suitcase and Sam laughed so hard she choked.

Alex's father cooked some spaghetti for an early supper, and while they all ate, they watched the birds pointedly ignoring each other. Then it was time for Sam and Margaret Trueblood to leave. Nobody knew what to say.

"I hate dragging out farewells," Margaret Trueblood said gruffly. "I'll wait for you in the car, Sam."

"Take good care of Bilbo," Sam muttered to Alex.

"I will. Write to me," Alex returned, but her voice cracked and it was hard to hear her.

Sam took a giant step toward her friend and hugged her hard. Then she charged off after Margaret to the waiting car.

The girls had made vague plans for meeting again next summer but that seemed terribly far away. Alex took a step after Sam and then stayed where she was.

The girls waved and kept waving at each other as the van rolled down the road. When she could no longer see the van, Alex went back in the house, moving slowly. Her feet were heavy and so was her heart, even with Bilbo and her father near at hand.

"Can I get you anything?" her father asked gently.

Alex swallowed and managed to speak in a husky voice.

"I think I'll lie down for a minute. I'm tired, I guess...."

She made it into her room and shut the door before she began to cry.

When she woke up, it was evening. She was covered with a quilt. And lying next to her pillow was a book by Dick King-Smith. It was called *Harry's Mad* and it was all about a boy named Harry and his incredible African Grey parrot. Alex began to read and found herself laughing. Taking it with her, she went out to find her father.

He was asleep in front of the television.

"Hell's bells," Bilbo said, proving he was as clever as Harry's talkative bird.

Alex grinned and went over to his cage.

"Want a head scratch?" she asked softly.

He bobbed his head up and down and fluffed up his neck feathers....

"Hurry up, George," he said.

The Truebloods' van left the neighbourhood where Jonathan Kennedy lived and headed for the highway. Before too long, Margaret and Sam were facing into the golden glow of the sunset. Sam blinked away not only the sun's dazzle but a mist of tears.

"Grow or wilt," Alex had said.

Well, Sam thought, as she rolled up the window, she would not take to wilting permanently but she certainly felt limp at the moment. Everything was ending. Her everyday and exciting friendship with Alex was over. Adults were in on it now, and the need to plot and keep their secret had passed. Now, if they got together again before September, they would have to ask permission and discuss plans with grown-ups who liked to keep their hands on the steering wheel. She sniffed.

"You're going to have a big job consoling Peony and Milkweed," Margaret said, her eyes on the road. "They grew very fond of Alex during the past weeks."

Sam straightened. Her spirits rose like a soaring kite. How had she forgotten the papillons? Alex had always been in charge of them and they had run to her as though she had won them, heart and soul. But now she would not be there. Maybe they would snuggle up with the real Sam.

"Rosie is due to whelp at the end of the week," the woman went on. "I'm running low on good names. If you'd be interested, you could christen the babies when they emerge. Alex's Sweet William is doing beautifully."

"I'd love to," Sam said huskily.

Flower names drifted through her head as they drove. Cornflower … Tulip … Daffodil … Lily. Hollyhock would be perfect for a girl. Summer flowers—to help her remember the summer just past when she had been somebody else.

If somebody calls out "Alex" tomorrow, she wondered, will I turn my head? Is there still a part of me that will always answer to that name?

She didn't know. She would find out, she supposed, but she was suddenly very tired. It had been a long day and her world had been turned upside-down again. She gazed out the car window at the evening sky. Its beauty rested her heart. The sun had slipped below the horizon, leaving the sky splashed with gold and amber and above that a soft wash of pale translucent green. When she tipped her head back and looked up, the sky above was a deep rich blue and in its depths, the first star was sending her some mysterious message.

"A penny for your thoughts," Margaret said softly.

But Sam could not put them into words. She wasn't thinking, not quite. She was coming back to herself, Sam, and leaving behind the excitement and confusion that had held her, like an enchantment, since she and Alex had met on the plane. It was a moment to feel, not to talk about.

Margaret Trueblood smiled and did not press her.

"I'm saying goodbye to Alex," Sam thought of telling her.

But she knew she wasn't. Alex Kennedy was her friend for life. It was the Alex inside her she was letting go of.

"Alice," she said. "Thomas called me Alice."

"I heard him," Margaret said.

"He'll be calling me Sam from now on," Sam whispered. "He'll forget Alice."

They drove on in silence until they reached the Guelph turnoff.

"It'll be all right," Margaret told her at last. She stretched out her hand and touched Sam's clenched fist, gently uncurling the fingers. "You can keep Alice and Sam both."

Then, all at once, Sam knew she was ready. She would not be needing Alice and neither would Thomas. She was her father's girl, Samantha Scott.

And Bethany had promised to let her ride Echo anytime.

And Kenneth was coming over tomorrow to play with the pups.

"How about Dogwood," she said joyously, "or Johnny-jump-up?"

Margaret Trueblood laughed out loud.

"Brilliant!" she said.